Cherished Legacy

Johnnie Alexander

AnniesFiction.com

Books in The Inn at Magnolia Harbor series

Library of Congress-in-Publication Data
Cherished Legacy / by Johnnie Alexander
p. cm.
I. Title
              2020938305

AnniesFiction.com
(800) 282-6643
The Inn at Magnolia Harbor™
Series Creator: Shari Lohner
Editor: Lorie Jones
Cover Illustrator: Bonnie Leick

10 11 12 13 14 | Printed in China | 9 8 7 6 5 4 3 2

Grace

Grace Porter tucked her nose into her sleeve, then poured another can of tomato juice over Winston's reeking red-tinted brown fur. The cans were supposed to go to the food pantry. Instead, the contents soaked into the unhappy shih tzu mix's coat. Hopefully, Winston had learned his lesson and would never tangle with a skunk again.

"Does this stuff really work?" Grace asked the thirtysomething man standing outside the open laundry room door. The horrid odor threatened to choke her with each breath she took.

"This website says tomato juice covers the smell." Clayton Lowe, clad in a Two Green Thumbs T-shirt and khaki shorts, skimmed the screen on his smartphone.

Grace grimaced. "Not yet it hasn't."

As Grace sprayed warm water into his fur, Winston whimpered and placed a dripping paw on the rim of the laundry sink.

"Don't try that cuteness on me." Grace gently placed Winston's paw into the deep sink. "I'm mad at you."

"I don't think he believes you," Clayton said.

"He never does." But when had Grace ever been truly mad at the lovable pooch? She couldn't remember even one time.

Clayton held up his phone, though he stood too far away for Grace to see what was on the screen. "I found a recipe on a website about dogs. Hydrogen peroxide, baking soda, and liquid dish detergent."

"I've got all that," she said. "Do you think it'll work?"

"I'd say it's worth a try." Clayton focused on his screen. "Several people have left positive comments on the post. Besides, all you've got to lose is eau de skunk." He chuckled at his own joke.

Grace laughed as she tried to push a stray lock of hair back with her upper arm. Her damp shirt clung to her skin, and tomato juice stained her fingers. Winston wasn't the only one getting an unwelcome bath. "I don't think I should go into the kitchen. Would you mind getting those things for me?"

"Always glad to help," he said.

Grace told Clayton where to find the products. While she waited for him to return, she rinsed the remaining tomato juice from Winston's fur. "I've never been more thankful for this sink," she said to him. At least the sickening odor would be confined to the laundry room.

She hoped.

Winston whimpered again, and Grace was sure his brown eyes were expressing his regret for his encounter with the strange black-and-white creature. Maybe he'd mistaken it for a cat, but she doubted he would ever do so again.

"It's okay. I forgive you," she murmured. Any reassuring hugs would have to wait until the stench was completely gone.

Clayton returned with a bowl of the de-skunking ingredients already mixed together. "I hate to tell you this, but someone's coming up the drive."

Grace checked the wall clock. "I hope it's not Kaydi Engstrom."

"A guest?"

"I wasn't expecting her for another hour." Grace frowned, unsure what to do. She owned the Magnolia Harbor Inn with her younger sister, Charlotte Wylde, who was at her cottage. It was located a short walk away on the property, but Grace didn't want to make a guest wait.

"I'll take care of Winston." Clayton stirred the concoction, then placed the bowl on the counter by the sink. "Go greet your guest."

"Like this?" Grace glanced down at her bath-splattered, juice-stained clothes and swept out her hands. Drops of water flew from her fingers. "You go."

Clayton handed her a clean towel with a shrug. "I'm just here to pull the weeds, ma'am," he said with an exaggerated drawl.

"And rescue Winston from skunks."

"Not soon enough."

"At least you tried. I suppose it could have been worse." Grace wiped her arms with the towel. "He's all yours."

She left by the back door and jogged around the three-story antebellum mansion. Hopefully, she'd reach the front veranda before her guest entered the inn. Rounding the corner, she tossed the towel behind a freestanding trellis covered with sweet-smelling yellow jessamine vines and made a mental note to retrieve it later.

"Welcome," she called to the woman standing near a parked taxi.

The woman turned to face her.

Grace blinked in disbelief, not sure if she could believe her own eyes. "Danielle? Is it really you?"

Fashionably dressed in casual pants and a short-sleeved top, Danielle Holloway removed her designer sunglasses and stared. "Hello, Grace." A slight smile lifted the corners of her mouth, but it didn't reach her eyes.

A warm flush crept up Grace's cheeks. Of all the people to see her looking like a mess. Danielle had been promoted to vice president of new business development at Maddox Creative after Grace resigned from the position, though she hadn't been Grace's choice to take her place.

She shook her head. This wasn't the time for a trip down memory lane—only a time to wish Winston hadn't chosen today to play with a feline impostor.

"We had an incident," Grace said apologetically, her mind racing to find an explanation for why Danielle was here and why she had arrived in a taxi.

"Nothing too serious, I hope." Danielle took a few steps forward, then wrinkled her nose and stopped.

Grace gave a self-conscious shrug. "My dog, Winston, met a skunk."

"Does that happen often?"

"Thankfully, no." Grace forced a smile. "What can I do for you?"

Danielle glanced at the mansion. "I know it seems odd for me to show up like this without calling first. Do you have a vacancy by any chance?"

"I do," Grace said, struggling to hide her surprise. Danielle lived in Charleston. Only an hour's drive away. So why hadn't she driven her own car? More to the point—why was she here at all? "We had a cancellation yesterday for the Buttercup Suite. It has a private bath and a lovely view of the lake."

"What about skunks?" Danielle asked, her eyes flickering with amusement.

"Not in any of the rooms," Grace replied. "That I can promise you."

"Great. I'll take it."

Grace almost offered to help with Danielle's bags. It was what she usually did for guests, but she didn't dare touch the designer luggage the driver was removing from the cab's trunk, not in her current state. She smiled at Danielle. "How long will you be staying?"

Danielle shifted her gaze away from Grace. "I'm not sure. Is that a problem?"

"That particular suite is booked for the week of the Fourth of July," Grace answered, "but you can stay there through next Sunday."

"That's fine." Danielle's voice held a fragile tone that shifted into haughtiness. "Shall we go in?"

"Please go ahead." Grace gestured toward the veranda stairs. "My sister, Charlotte, will be here in a few minutes to help you get settled. It's a beautiful suite. I know you'll be comfortable."

"Thank you. There's no need for her to rush," Danielle said, then addressed the cabdriver. "I would appreciate your help with my luggage."

After grabbing her bags, he followed her up the stairs and into the foyer.

Grace sighed heavily and pulled her phone from her back pocket. She sent a quick text to Charlotte, then picked up the towel. A fresh whiff of skunk odor overpowered the delicate fragrance of the golden flowers and assaulted her nose.

As she returned to the laundry room, Grace prayed Clayton's solution had worked on Winston, especially since she needed a proper de-skunking too. She shuddered at the thought of bathing in the ingredients.

When she opened the back door, Winston raced toward her and jumped into her arms.

How strange. Clayton was nowhere to be seen.

2

Kaydi

Kaydi Engstrom quickly saw that the gorgeous Wisteria Loft Suite, tucked away on the third floor of the delightful Magnolia Harbor Inn, was too luxurious for words. The view of the lake took her breath away. So had the welcome she'd received from the owners, Grace and Charlotte. The two women had brimmed over with genuine Southern hospitality. The entire place was even more amazing than Kaydi had dared to dream.

Even though she'd spent most of the day in airports, thanks to a delayed flight during a long layover in Atlanta, her spirits weren't at all frayed, nor was she tired. She was eager to attend the evening's hospitality hour and begin her sleuthing. Kaydi was determined to find out whatever she could about Callie Jo Emmett Piper, her grandmother.

First she took a shower to freshen up, then dressed in one of the darling new outfits she'd bought for this adventure. A lovely thrift store find, the floral dress had still had the designer tags attached when Kaydi purchased it. Such a bargain.

She didn't have any idea why anyone purchased such gorgeous clothes only to donate them to charity, but their loss was her gain. Finding cast-off treasures in thrift stores, pawnshops, and estate sales was her hobby and her passion. When it came to old jewelry, it was also one of her sources of income.

Kaydi added a chunky necklace she'd created with the blue and green stones from an antique brooch and slipped an assortment of gold

and silver rings on her fingers. After strapping on wedged sandals, she
went downstairs and out to the veranda.

"Welcome," Grace said warmly. "I'm so glad you joined us."

"I wouldn't have missed it for the world." Kaydi glanced at the
refreshment table. An assortment of appetizers, including caprese
skewers and chicken lettuce wraps, were artfully arranged on festive
platters. The selections were perfect for a sun-drenched June day.
"Everything looks amazingly scrumptious."

"Charlotte is a professional chef and the author of several best-
selling cookbooks." Grace smiled in her sister's direction. "She always
creates wonderful hors d'oeuvres for our guests."

"I can't wait to try them," Kaydi said.

"Can I get you something to drink?" Grace asked. "We have white
wine, sweet tea, and chilled lemonade."

"I'll take a glass of sweet tea, please." Kaydi almost bubbled over
inside. She couldn't believe she was really here and about to taste
authentic Southern sweet tea for the first time in her life. According
to her grandmother, nothing tasted as good on a sultry day.

Grace poured the tea into a tall glass. "We added lemon juice and
fresh mint to the ice cubes. I hope you like it."

"Sounds positively delicious." Kaydi sipped the drink and let the
cold tea wash over her taste buds. "It is."

Grace laughed. "I'm glad you think so. Please help yourself to
the refreshments."

As Kaydi filled her plate, a petite woman who appeared to be in
her late sixties arrived.

Grace greeted the newcomer with a hug, then ushered her over to
the table. "Kaydi, I'd like you to meet Winnie Bennett. She's my aunt,
and she lives nearby." She turned to Winnie. "This is Kaydi Engstrom.
She's here all the way from Omaha."

"How nice to meet you." Winnie's hazel eyes sparkled with warmth. "Did you drive or fly?"

"I flew. What an adventure it was trying to find my way around the airport in Atlanta. Our flight was delayed, which was a good thing. Otherwise, I might have missed it." Kaydi giggled. "I'm sorry. I do tend to go on sometimes, but it's been a marvelous day. My parents told me the flight would be awful, but that wasn't true. I had the greatest time talking to my seatmates."

Winnie smiled. "I imagine they enjoyed talking with you too."

Without a doubt, the older woman was a kindred spirit. Kaydi liked her immediately.

Grace excused herself to welcome a couple with two young boys. The children were wrapped in beach towels, and the mom carried a colorful tote. She shooed the boys indoors with a promise to Grace that they'd come back as soon as they had changed.

"Are you in South Carolina on vacation?" Winnie asked, pulling Kaydi's attention from the family. "Or business?"

"I suppose you could say vacation," Kaydi said with a bright smile. "I've never ventured this far from home before, but once I found this lovely inn online, I made a reservation, packed my bags, got on my very first flight, and here I am."

Winnie gave her a quizzical look. "Would it be too nosy if I asked why you chose to come to Magnolia Harbor out of all the places you could have gone?"

"Not at all," Kaydi said, keeping her tone light. She wasn't ready to reveal her true purpose for coming here. Not even to a kindred spirit. She needed more information first. "I guess you could say it was a whim."

That wasn't really a lie. Using most of her savings to make this trip and hopping on a plane had been a whim. And maybe it was a foolish one. Only time would tell. But what did Kaydi have to lose? Nothing really. Even if she didn't discover what she hoped to, she'd return with wondrous memories of her time here. She was sure of that.

"A whim?" Winnie echoed. "I like that. It takes spunk to make a spur-of-the-moment decision like that."

"I've never thought of myself as spunky." Quite the opposite, in fact. Though it was true Kaydi had always skipped to a different tune than most people. Her parents hadn't seemed to know what to do about that, but her grandmother had understood. She'd apparently followed her own whim way back in the day. If only she'd been able to tell Kaydi more of the story.

Kaydi shook away the distressing thoughts before she wandered too far along that difficult trail and focused on Winnie. "Have you always lived in Magnolia Harbor?"

"I moved here after I married my high school sweetheart." Winnie leaned forward as if to share a secret. "That was almost fifty years ago."

"How wonderful," Kaydi remarked. Her grandparents hadn't been lucky enough to reach that milestone. Again, Kaydi forced away her gloomy thoughts. She was the heroine of her own adventure, and she planned to make the most of it. This wasn't the time for mourning. "Fifty years is a long time."

"I suppose it seems so to someone as young as you," Winnie said. "For Gus and me, the years have flown by quicker than we could have ever imagined."

"Is he still your sweetheart?" Kaydi teased. "I'm guessing yes."

"You'd be guessing right." Winnie laughed. "There's no better man out there."

"I hope to meet someone like that." Kaydi gave a wistful sigh. "I'm determined to marry only for the deepest possible love. Just like Elizabeth Bennet."

Good humor brightened Winnie's already pleasant smile. "You're a Jane Austen fan?"

"I am, though my favorite is actually *Persuasion*," Kaydi said. "When Captain Wentworth and Anne Elliot finally get together at the end, I always swoon."

"It's one of my favorites too." Winnie picked up a plate and added a few fresh peach slices to it. "Perhaps you'll meet your Captain Wentworth here at the inn. We've had our share of romances over the years."

"Really?"

Winnie nodded. "In fact, just this past Valentine's Day, the granddaughter of the mansion's previous owners came for a visit. She and one of our local men got reacquainted, and the sparks flew."

"That's so romantic." To find deep, abiding love in such an incredible place—it would be like a fairy tale come true. However, Kaydi had a different purpose for staying at the inn. She was determined not to get sidetracked.

"I don't see anything like that happening to me," she said. Maybe now was the time to throw out a bit of bait. "I'm interested in the local history. This must have been a glorious estate at one time."

"I'm sure it was, but that would have been a long time ago." Winnie added a few more snacks to her plate, then gestured toward a nearby table.

The women took their plates and sat down across from each other.

"These big homes are expensive to maintain," Winnie continued. "When the owners of this place passed away, the house and practically everything in it went to auction."

"That's so sad," Kaydi said. "Didn't the granddaughter want the mansion?"

"I think deep in her heart she dreamed of living here, but God seems to have had other plans for her life. She's very happy with the renovations Grace and Charlotte have made, and she seems to know the inn is in good hands with them."

"Still, it must be hard to lose a family home as impressive as this one," Kaydi said.

"You're seeing it after all the improvements have been made," Winnie told her. "My nieces worked hard to restore it."

Kaydi took a sip of the refreshing tea. What if this estate was the one? Maybe she could learn more about the granddaughter from Winnie, but she had to be careful. She didn't want the older woman to become suspicious of Kaydi's true intent. She chose a different tack. "How many other estates are in the area?" she asked, trying to sound casual even as her heart started beating faster.

"Unfortunately, not many. Most of the old houses have been torn down to make way for new construction. If you want to know more about the area and its history, you should visit the Heritage Library."

"That's a great idea. Where is it?"

"Downtown Magnolia Harbor on Willow Street," Winnie answered. "It's a block over from Main Street in the historic district. Talk to Phyllis Gendel, the head librarian. She'll be able to help you."

"Heritage Library. Willow Street. Phyllis Gendel." Kaydi nodded firmly. "I've got it."

"You could visit the Jackson House Museum too," Winnie added. "Make sure you also talk to Julep Buckley. She used to be the president of the historical society, so she's a walking history lesson when it comes to Magnolia Harbor's past. Would you like her phone number?"

"She won't mind if I call?" Kaydi asked, surprised.

"Not at all. Julep loves company, and she loves this town." Winnie smiled. "Just give yourself plenty of time to visit because she'll have many wonderful stories to share."

Kaydi's heart fluttered. She'd never expected to get so many resources so quickly. She had only arrived a few hours ago. "You are the absolute best," she enthused. "I really appreciate it."

"Glad to be of help." Winnie dug through her bag, pulled out her phone, and forwarded Julep's contact info to Kaydi's cell. "That's Julep's home phone number. She prefers it to a cell."

"Thank you."

When Winnie returned her phone to her bag, her smile broadened. "Look what I found." She held up an unopened pack of butter rum Life Savers. "These are for you," she announced, placing the roll in Kaydi's palm.

Startled, Kaydi tried to return them. "No, I can't take your candy."

"Don't be silly," Winnie said. "Unless you don't like butter rum."

"I'm not sure I've ever had them."

"All the more reason for you to take them then." Winnie closed Kaydi's hand around the roll. "Keep them with you. You never know when they'll come in handy."

"Thank you." What else could she say? Kaydi didn't want the candy, but she couldn't be rude. She slipped them into her bag. "You're very kind."

"I need to go home and see my high school sweetheart," Winnie said as she stood. "I sure hope you enjoy your stay here and that you learn everything you want to know about our little corner of the world."

"I hope so too," Kaydi said.

Winnie started to turn away, then hesitated. "I just remembered. There's an estate sale at the Norwood mansion tomorrow."

Kaydi's pulse quickened. Could this be the place she was searching for? That would be way too cool. Even if it wasn't, she couldn't pass up the potential treasures to be found at an estate sale. "That sounds interesting. Do you know the address?"

"Do you have a car?" Winnie asked.

"I picked up a rental in Charleston."

"Follow Lake Haven Road through town and around the other side of the lake," Winnie said. "Then watch for the signs. They'll lead you there."

"Great. I'll do that."

After a quick goodbye and a wave in Kaydi's direction, Winnie disappeared into the house.

Kaydi wasn't sure what to think of the older woman—except that she liked her. Talk about spunk and energy. Winnie reminded Kaydi of her grandmother. At least before the dementia had cloaked her grandma's true personality.

Winnie had been helpful. Now Kaydi had three resources: the library, the Jackson House Museum, and Julep Buckley, which was such a perfect name for a Southern matriarch. She'd start with the library, then give Julep a call. Hopefully, by this time tomorrow, Kaydi would discover the truth about her family tree.

The couple returned with their young boys, who had changed into shorts and T-shirts, and Grace introduced them to Kaydi.

For the rest of the social hour, Kaydi visited with Chet and Mandy Zema and their energetic sons, ten-year-old Robbie and seven-year-old Henry. They had been vacationing at the inn every summer since it opened, and they normally stayed in the Rosebud and Bluebell Suites, which shared a large bathroom.

Grace had mentioned Jack and Melissa Hayes from Michigan, who were staying in the Dogwood Suite. The young couple was spending the day in Charleston and wouldn't return until late this evening.

Kaydi hoped to meet them at breakfast the next day. Oh, what fun she was already having, and this was only the first day of her spontaneous, whimsical, all-on-her-own trip.

How could it possibly get any better?

3

Grace

After breakfast the next morning, Winnie entered the kitchen through the back entry as Grace put the last coffee cup in the dishwasher. The spry older woman lived less than a mile from the inn and often stopped by on her daily walk.

"Usually I'm on time to help you clean up, but I got a call from Missy," Winnie said. "She's in an uproar about plans for the Fourth of July parade. I think I calmed her down."

Missy Perkins, the director of the local chamber of commerce, had a personality as flamboyant as her red bouffant hair and false eyelashes.

"I can't say I blame her," Grace said. "We just had a festival last month. It seems there's little time to rest before we're planning the next event in town."

"Am I too late for a second breakfast?" Winnie perched on one of the stools at the marble island.

"Our guests seemed eager to start their weekend, so they finished breakfast early." Grace placed a tray of fruit skewers and a basket of assorted pastries in front of her aunt. "But I set aside a few goodies for you. Coffee?"

"Please." Winnie selected a fruit skewer with melon chunks and grapes, then added half a bagel to her plate. "What about you? Any big weekend plans?"

Grace forced a smile, though she knew her feigned cheer wouldn't fool her aunt. At least Winnie and Charlotte both had seemed to come to an unspoken agreement not to bring up the dreaded subject of Hank, her ex-husband. She had believed that Hank had died in a tragic train accident more than twenty years ago, but he recently showed up on her doorstep alive and well. After missing the train, Hank had taken the opportunity to start a new life without the responsibilities of marriage and fatherhood.

If Grace wanted to talk about Hank, Winnie and Charlotte would gladly listen, but it was up to her to take that step. She didn't know if it was a step she'd ever be ready to take. *Time heals all wounds*, they said. Time would heal this one. She recalled a twisted version of the adage: *Time wounds all heels*.

Grace smiled to herself, but the thought wasn't funny. She didn't want to wound Hank, and she didn't wish him ill. But her ex-husband definitely was a heel—worse than a heel—and if his own actions created unhappy consequences for him, she wouldn't be surprised.

"Would you like to join us?" Winnie asked, breaking into Grace's reverie.

Grace startled. "I'm sorry. I didn't mean to ignore you. Guess I got lost in my own thoughts."

"There's nothing wrong with daydreaming," Winnie said in an offhand manner, but concern darkened her eyes.

"I'm fine," Grace said firmly. She poured coffee into a mug and set it on the island. "What were you saying?"

"Only that Gus and I are going to Roy's farm this afternoon. See what bounties we can find there." Roy Bevins and his wife, Gladys, sold organic fruits and vegetables, free-range chickens, and their own cheeses at their farm located on the outskirts of Magnolia Harbor. "Would you like to drive out with us? There's plenty of room in Gus's car."

"Sounds like fun, but I think I'll stick around here today." Grace added a detergent pod to the dishwasher and closed the door. "Charlotte and Dean are going to a seafood festival on the coast. She left a few minutes before you arrived to get ready."

"I'm surprised Dean can leave town on a Saturday," Winnie remarked. "Aren't there Little League games today?"

"The team that he coaches is playing this morning." Grace found it pleasantly surprising how much Dean, who seemed to relish bachelorhood, enjoyed coaching young children, and the parents loved having their children on Dean's team. His brother, who lived in Atlanta, had ten-year-old twin boys. Dean—the head chef and owner of The Tidewater inn and restaurant across Lake Haven—didn't get to see them as much as he would like, so perhaps coaching was his way of making up for missing them.

Grace grabbed her mug and joined Winnie at the island. "He and Charlotte are leaving as soon as the game is over. I'm sure they'll bring fresh fish home with them, so you'll want to be here tonight for hospitality hour. I can only imagine what Charlotte will come up with to serve our guests."

"Speaking of guests, I enjoyed talking to Kaydi last night," Winnie said. "She certainly was full of questions."

"What kind of questions?" Grace asked.

"All about the inn. About Magnolia Harbor. I suggested she visit the library and talk to Julep."

"How interesting. She reminded me of a kid in a candy store when she checked in." Grace took a sip of coffee. "The drive from the Charleston airport was an adventure. The inn was the most beautiful place she'd ever seen. The flowers in her room were gorgeous."

"She does seem to have a remarkable zest for life. As every young woman should." Winnie's eyes sparkled with curiosity. "Though after I left her, I couldn't help wondering if she was here on some type of quest."

"We've had our share of those over the years, haven't we?" Grace toyed with her coffee cup. "Adopted children searching for clues to their heritage. Crushed hearts seeking another chance at love." She winced. Why had she said that?

Why couldn't she get thoughts of Hank out of her mind?

Her own heart was bruised after his sudden appearance. The conversation she'd had with Spencer Lewis had been even worse. Just as she was growing closer to her handsome neighbor, she'd learned she wasn't a widow after all. She'd had to squash her feelings. It was so much easier said than done.

After the difficult and unusual experience Grace had been through, how could she give her heart to anyone? She needed time to get used to the idea that she wasn't a widow but a divorcee. Both labels meant she'd once been married and was now single. However, the emotions they created weren't the same. It was as if she had to redefine herself by sorting through all the years since she'd gotten the news of Hank's supposed death and changing the prism of how she'd lived through them. She didn't have that much energy, but ignoring the pull to do so created its own tension.

"Maybe Kaydi is an investigative journalist," Winnie said in a light tone.

Dear Aunt Winnie. Grace loved her for trying to distract her from her sad thoughts. For her sake, she'd play along. "What do you suppose she's investigating?"

"Who knows?" Winnie took a long sip of her coffee. "Perhaps Charlotte is a double agent. Perhaps I am."

"And perhaps I'm an evil mastermind about to take over the world," Grace joked.

"Not you, my dear. You don't have an evil bone in your body." Winnie spread a thin layer of strawberry-flavored cream cheese on her bagel. "Do you think Kaydi could be one of those secret shoppers?

You know, the ones who go into places and write up reports about the service they receive and how well they were treated?"

"If she was doing that, she wouldn't have asked so many questions." Grace furrowed her brow. "Maybe she's a writer. We've had our share of those too."

"We could speculate all day. I suppose we'll know when she tells us."

"*If* she tells us."

The women chatted several more minutes, then walked outside so Grace could cut fresh flowers for the front desk.

Winston followed them, his tail wagging in delight. The slight scent of dish detergent wafted from his thick coat.

Danielle emerged from the rose garden.

Grace smiled and waved at her guest.

Danielle returned Grace's wave, then wandered in the other direction.

"I think she's avoiding us," Grace said.

"She looks familiar," Winnie said. "Who is she?"

"Danielle Holloway. You may have met her once or twice. She works at Maddox Creative."

"She was at The Book Cottage yesterday." Winnie stopped to inspect the leaves on a nearby rosebush. "I thought I knew her, but I couldn't remember her name or where I'd seen her before."

"She should know you too. Didn't she say anything?"

"I got the idea she was embarrassed to be seen." Winnie moved to the next bush. "There was a man with her, but when she saw me, her face turned all shades of red. He disappeared, and she pulled a thick book from the shelves and started flipping the pages. I sensed she didn't want to talk to me, so I didn't approach her."

"That seems odd." Grace cut the stem of a fragrant pink rose from one of her favorite bushes.

"I thought so too." Winnie laughed self-consciously. "I hung around until after she left, and then I went to see what she'd been reading. It was a book on military strategy in the Middle Ages. It didn't seem that interesting."

"Oh, what a thing for you to do," Grace teased.

The women chuckled.

When Grace returned to her task, she couldn't stop thinking about Danielle. She hadn't attended last night's hospitality hour, nor had she appeared for breakfast this morning. Now it seemed she had purposely gone out of her way to avoid speaking to them. "Maybe she's doing research for a marketing campaign."

"Do you miss it?" Winnie asked.

The unexpected question took Grace aback. "Marketing campaigns? Not at all." She surveyed the gardens, the inn, and the lake. "I'd never give all this up to go back to that world. Danielle is welcome to it."

Danielle had not been Grace's choice for her replacement. The woman had seemed a bit shady, and Grace had someone else in mind to take over. Something had happened—internal politics, she supposed—and Danielle was offered the job. Grace's protégé resigned a few months later to take a position in Knoxville.

Now Danielle was here. In Magnolia Harbor. It all seemed so strange.

"I wonder who the man was," Grace mused, then held up her hand. "I know it's none of my business."

"I didn't get a good look at him, and I'm curious, especially now that I know who Danielle is." Winnie took the basket from Grace and straightened the flowers she'd already cut. "Usually, a secret rendezvous suggests a romantic tryst, but I don't believe that was the case."

"Why not?"

"Until I inadvertently interrupted them, they were very focused on their conversation. As if one was trying to persuade the other of something."

"I doubt we'll ever know what it was all about," Grace said, checking on Winston. He seemed to be happily engaged with chasing butterflies this morning. "Danielle and I were never close."

So why, out of all the places to stay in the area, had Danielle come here? She knew Grace owned the Magnolia Harbor Inn. Was she in some kind of trouble?

"If she needs my help, I wish she'd ask for it," Grace continued. "I'd do what I could."

"I know you would," Winnie reassured her. "For now, I think she wants to be left alone. We need to respect her wishes."

"You're right," Grace said as she cut a few roses for her aunt.

After Winnie went home, Grace strolled through the gardens to select a combination of daisies and ferns. As much as she tried to delight in the lovely blossoms and heady fragrances, Danielle kept intruding into her thoughts. Grace's intuition told her that Danielle wasn't here for a getaway from work. Something else was behind her sudden appearance. While Grace didn't want to get mired in any situation Danielle might be involved with, she also wanted to be a friend if Danielle needed one.

I don't know what's going on, Father, but You do. If I can assist Danielle, then guide her to confide in me. Help me to set aside any ill feelings I still have toward her. Please give me strength.

4

Danielle

The Buttercup Suite, with its king-size bed covered in sumptuous linens, an enchanting view of the lake, and a private bath, was both a haven and a prison.

Perhaps it had been a mistake to come here, but when Ace had told Danielle that he'd found refuge in Magnolia Harbor, she'd had no choice. The two of them needed to be near each other until the storm rolling over them passed by.

If only she knew when that would happen. The days since the discovery of the theft seemed to drag, the hours slogging like thick molasses from a chilled jar.

The only blessing—and even it was a mixed one—was Grace. In a way, Ace couldn't have chosen a better place to hide. As soon as he'd contacted Danielle, she'd remembered that her former colleague had opened a bed-and-breakfast in the small town after leaving Maddox Creative. Even though Danielle and Grace had their differences, Danielle sensed a tug she couldn't explain that urged her to find refuge at the inn.

She hadn't expected to find Grace in such a disheveled state—she'd never seen the woman appear anything but collected. Though Grace probably felt Danielle was always collected too. If only Grace could see the turmoil inside Danielle's spirit.

Danielle pressed her hand against her stomach, but the gesture did little to settle her nerves. Maybe she should confide in Grace. She'd thought about doing so this morning when she saw Grace walking out to the flower garden, but then she'd realized Grace wasn't alone. An older woman was with her, the same woman who had seen Danielle and Ace in the bookstore.

Grace's aunt.

Danielle didn't remember the woman's name, but they'd met a couple of times at the company's family events when Grace was still with Maddox Creative.

Ace had run out of the bookstore as soon as he noticed the aunt watching them. If only Danielle had been able to talk to him for a few more moments. She could have tried to persuade him to seek the help they needed, not that it would have done any good. He was too frightened of what might happen. He needed time.

Danielle heaved a deep and heavy sigh. It was hard to believe that she was embroiled in such a predicament.

When Ace had called Danielle to break the news, she'd acted like a crazy person. As soon as she had hung up, she quickly packed her bags, drove south to Savannah, Georgia, took a train back north to the small town of Denmark, South Carolina, called a taxi to drive her to nearby Snellville, and took another taxi to the inn.

A memory verse she'd learned a long time ago in Sunday school whirled around her head the entire time she traveled from one place to another on her circuitous journey. *The wicked flee when no one is pursuing.*

Except she wasn't wicked, and neither was Ace.

If no one was pursuing—a big and frightening *if*—then their overreaction was ridiculous.

The stakes were too high to risk not overreacting, and the consequences were unknown. Their best option—their only option—was to lie low until they could figure out a better plan.

Perhaps she could share all this turmoil with Grace. When

she worked at Maddox, she had a reputation for levelheadedness and compassion.

But Danielle couldn't talk to Grace without Ace's go-ahead, and he wasn't ready to share their troubles. He was too afraid of the potential ramifications to trust anyone.

For now, Danielle needed to stay cooped up in her haven. Her prison.

She picked up a novel she'd bought at the Savannah train station and adjusted the pillows on the wide bed. If only she was here on vacation as she'd told Grace. The tastefully decorated suite would be a great place for a personal retreat. Maybe someday she could come back and relax in its comfort.

Danielle found her place in the story and started to read. When she reached a new chapter without any idea of what had happened in the last one, she closed the book. She'd hoped to get lost in the popular novel, widely regarded as a page-turning thriller, but how could she get lost in someone else's problems when she was dealing with her own real-life thriller story?

After tossing the book onto the bed, she grabbed her phone. She somehow needed to persuade Ace that they couldn't do this on their own. They needed to confide in someone.

She tapped the screen to call him and prayed he'd be able to talk.

"Hey." Ace's voice sounded warm, but there was also a hint of worry in his tone. "Is everything okay?"

"I'm fine. How are you doing?"

"Working hard." He blew out a breath. "I'm not accustomed to this kind of physical labor."

Danielle closed her eyes. The poor guy usually worked with his mind, not his muscles. "Why are you doing it? You could hole up somewhere. Think of it as a vacation."

"If I did that, I'd go crazy," Ace responded. "At least I'm getting more exercise than I did sitting behind a desk."

"Do you miss crunching numbers?" Danielle asked. The conversation wasn't going the way she wanted, but she wouldn't get anywhere by pushing him too hard too fast.

"Honestly? Not as much as I thought I would."

"What if this thing isn't resolved and you can't go back?" Danielle walked over to the window. The clear water of Lake Haven sparkled beneath the brilliance of the June sun. Colorful kayaks bobbed amidst the rippling waves.

"I'm not sure I care." Ace paused, but Danielle didn't fill the silence. He let out a deep breath. "What about you?"

"Marketing is all I know. It's what I love." As Danielle said it, she wondered if it was still true.

"Hopefully we'll figure out a way to return to our normal lives."

She turned from the window and perched on the edge of the upholstered chair angled near the fireplace. This was the opening she needed. "Not on our own."

"Dannie—"

"We have to confide in someone. At least I do."

Something tightened in his voice. "Why?"

"Just to clear my thoughts. To get someone else's perspective." She leaned into the chair's comfort and pulled her legs close to her chest. "To figure out if there's something we can do. Something we haven't thought about."

"You have someone in mind." It wasn't a question.

Danielle hugged her knees and took a deep breath. "The woman who owns the inn. She used to work at Maddox Creative. In fact, I took her place when she left."

"You mean Grace Porter. I know her."

"Then you know she's a good person. She'll understand what we're up against."

Again, silence.

Don't say anything. Let him think.

Another heavy sigh came through the line. "I can't. Not yet."

She imagined him lowering his head, the way he always did when they disagreed. As if retreating into himself and silently asking for an apology at the same time. He probably didn't even realize he did it, which made the gesture all the more endearing.

In different circumstances . . .

Danielle tried to swallow the lump threatening to choke her. She couldn't break down. Not now. That wouldn't do either of them any good. "When?" The word came out as soft as a breath. Too soft for him to hear?

Finally, Ace spoke. "I don't know. It's too risky."

"I'm scared."

"Me too."

"Can we get together?" she asked. "Talk about this in person?"

"I want to, but I need time to think things through."

"That's all we've been doing." The uncharacteristic sharpness in her voice startled her. She rubbed her temple and softened her tone. "Please give me something to hold on to. A little bit of hope."

"I can't. I just—" His voice cracked. "Stay safe, and I'll talk to you soon."

The call disconnected before she could respond.

Danielle dropped the phone onto the chair and hurried to the bathroom. With her palms pressed against the vanity, she leaned over the sink and sobbed. She'd only been doing her job, and he had only been doing his. How had everything gone so wrong?

For reasons she didn't completely understand, an innocent man was being accused of something he hadn't done, and her head was also on the chopping block.

No matter what Ace said, they needed help. She had to persuade him to confide in someone.

Though she couldn't explain why, she knew beyond a shadow of a doubt that that someone was Grace Porter.

Luke

The sprawling Norwood mansion sat on wooded acreage about a hundred feet off the main road. Luke Brannick wandered past the long tables set up on the front lawn toward the outbuildings. Back in the day, the barn had housed a few horses on one side and stored equipment on the other. Sometime in the last century, it had become the family's garage.

Now the family was gone. The last resident, Charles Norwood, had finally been persuaded to move to an assisted-living facility on the outskirts of Atlanta. It was easier for his son to keep an eye on him, and Charles had the opportunity to spend more time with his grandchildren.

A win-win situation.

And yet Luke couldn't help feeling a sense of loss. The Norwoods had lived on this property for more than a hundred years. Now all their possessions—items that had once held value to someone in the family—were spread out on tables for strangers to paw through, haggle over, and cart away.

Fortunately, it wasn't only strangers. Neighbors and friends just like him were here too, seeking out bargains with a bit of history. He was searching for the unusual, something old to transform into something new—a sculpture he could create to fit into that odd corner in the Townsends' backyard.

Blanche Townsend had commissioned Luke to create something special for her husband's upcoming birthday. She owned the local bookstore, The Book Cottage, and Wesley was a lieutenant at the

Magnolia Harbor Police Department. His grandparents and their families had been farmers, and Blanche had asked Luke to create something that would honor that heritage.

If not for the commission, Luke wouldn't be at this estate sale. The run-down and forsaken homes, even ones as modest as this one, cut too close for comfort.

Luke meandered through an assortment of lawn equipment, chatting with others who'd come to find a bargain. As he glanced up from inspecting a horse-drawn plow from the Civil War era, a young woman wearing blue-checked shorts and a pastel T-shirt caught his eye. She appeared puzzled as she examined an old sugarcane crusher.

A familiar tingle raced up Luke's spine. The antique crusher would be the perfect centerpiece for the Townsends' sculpture, and the young woman practically took his breath away. He joined her and cleared his throat to get her attention.

The woman faced him, and Luke found himself falling into the depths of the most gorgeous brown eyes he'd ever seen. Rounded cheeks, reddened by the June sun, and a dusting of freckles were framed by brown hair streaked with blonde and cut into an angular style.

Her dazzling smile sent his senses into a tailspin. It was all he could do not to clutch his chest to calm the sudden onslaught of a rapid beating he'd never experienced before. The beat sounded so loud to his ears that he could only hope she didn't hear it too.

"Do you have any idea what this is?" she asked.

"It's a sugarcane crusher." His voice cracked, and he cleared his throat again. Luke pointed to the various parts as he explained how the machine worked. "The sugarcane was placed here and crushed by these rollers. The juice was used to make syrup." He lowered his voice to a conspiratorial whisper. "Maybe even rum."

"That's interesting," she said. "I've never seen anything quite like it before. How do you know so much about it?" Now it was her turn to whisper. "Are you a rumrunner?"

"No, I'm not." Luke gave a self-conscious grin. "But I specialize in knowing obscure trivia. Like a jack-of-all-trades but master of none."

"A fine thing to be, I think." She extended her hand. "I'm Kaydi Engstrom."

Luke took her hand but didn't shake it. Her touch sent electric currents up his arm, down his spine, and into his toes. He didn't let go. "It's nice to meet you, Katie."

Her gaze darted to their hands, but she didn't pull away. She looked straight into his eyes and grinned. "Not Katie. K-A-Y-D-I. Kaydi."

"Kay. Dee." He emphasized the two syllables. "That's different. I've never met a Kaydi before."

She held up her free hand. "Oh, just wait."

For as long as you want. Luke still held her hand, and she didn't seem to mind. In fact, she exuded a strange sort of innocence as if she hadn't been hurt much by the world and didn't expect to be.

"There's more," Kaydi said, her eyes twinkling with mischief.

"More what?" he asked.

"More to my name. I won't tell you until you tell me yours, though."

"Sorry." He placed his free hand on both of theirs. Their palms were now damp with sweat. Why did the sun have to be so hot today? "I'm Luke Brannick."

"Native or tourist?" she asked.

"I'm a native. I've lived here all my life except when I was away at college. I went to Clemson and got a business degree." Luke winced, chiding himself for relaying his life story. "You're definitely a tourist."

"What makes you so sure?" Kaydi asked.

"Because I know almost everybody around here, and I've never seen you before."

"You're right." She glanced at their hands, but she still didn't pull away. "I'm staying at the Magnolia Harbor Inn."

Luke nodded. "Out on Lake Haven Road. It's a great place."

"Hey, Luke." Patrick Haney, the owner of Haney Auctions and Estate Sales, approached them. He nodded toward Kaydi, glanced at their clasped hands, then pasted on a huge smile and gestured toward the crusher. "Are you folks interested in this?"

"I don't think I'll be needing sugarcane juice anytime soon, and I have no idea how to make rum." Kaydi directed that mischievous grin at Luke.

Luke returned her smile and reluctantly let go of her hand. "In that case, I think I might find a use for it. What's the asking price?"

Patrick named an amount, which Luke countered. Patrick suggested a compromise, and Luke agreed. He probably could have gotten the crusher for less—he doubted anyone else here was interested in it—but he wanted to close the transaction before Kaydi got bored and wandered away. Money wasn't his primary concern at the moment.

"Can I pick it up later?" Luke asked as he shook Patrick's hand, cementing the deal. "I rode my motorcycle over here."

"Sure thing." Patrick wrote Luke's name on a tag and attached it to the item. "If anything else catches your fancy, let me know."

His fancy had certainly been caught. Luke glanced at Kaydi, who stood a few feet away. She appeared totally engrossed with another antique contraption. It resembled a small trough on legs with a scrubbing board at one end.

As if she sensed his eyes upon her, she smiled at him. "Is this a washing machine?"

"A gold star to the young lady," Patrick said enthusiastically before Luke could respond. "Now I know you wouldn't want to trust your laundry to something like this, but imagine what it would look like as a planter. Quite unique, wouldn't you say?"

"Definitely unique," Kaydi agreed. "I'm afraid it's not for me."

Patrick wasn't one to give up at the first objection. He grabbed the handle by the wringer rollers to demonstrate how the washer worked.

Kaydi, obviously amused, gave it a try.

Luke shook his head and spied a tall metal implement built into a stand. That artistic tingling returned. "What's this?" he called to Patrick.

The three of them surrounded the item.

"A post driver." Patrick pointed to the bottom of the stand. "You hook your mules to these runners and place the driver over the post. Give it two or three whacks, and the job's done. Drag, pull, or bribe your mules to the next spot, and do it all again. I've heard it said two men and their mules could cover about three-fourths of a mile in a day with this baby."

"That doesn't sound like much," Kaydi said.

"More than a man could do on his own," Patrick replied.

Luke walked around the post driver, running his fingers along the metal and scrutinizing its condition. A vision slowly came together in his imagination. This could provide the structural skeleton, the background, for the crusher. He'd weld the pieces together and—

"How much?" he asked.

"What are you going to do with it?" Patrick asked.

"Not sure." Luke tapped his head. "I can't quite see it yet."

Patrick took Luke's arm and drew him a few feet away. "We both know you overpaid for the crusher." He glanced over his shoulder at Kaydi. "I understand why, so I'm giving you a deal on the driver. My absolute rock-bottom price." He named the amount.

Luke made a show of considering, then agreed.

Patrick slapped him on the back and wrote his name on another tag.

"Was that really your lowest price?" Luke asked as Patrick made out an invoice for both items.

Patrick laughed. "No, but I won't charge you for delivery. Now go have fun with your new friend."

Luke placed the invoice in his pocket, trying to ignore the heat creeping up his neck. "Thanks."

They returned to Kaydi.

Patrick attached the tag to the driver. "The church youth group is selling lemonade freezes by the front porch. Be sure and get yourselves one before you leave." He walked away to help another potential customer.

"I could use a cold drink after all that dickering," Luke said. "How about I treat you to one?"

Kaydi tilted her head, and a small smile lifted the corners of her lips. "Dickering? I think you may be an easy mark," she teased.

Luke chuckled. She was right, but he'd been too distracted by her presence to bargain. "I'll get the best of him next time."

"I'm sure you will." She tucked her arm into his. "I'd love a lemonade freeze."

Luke couldn't have been more thrilled if someone had handed him a check for a million dollars. He'd heard about moments like this, and he had seen instant attraction happen in the movies, but he'd never believed they were real. He had definitely never expected to experience something like that for himself.

Together he and Kaydi strolled toward the stand, stopping to examine a few other items along the way.

"So what did you mean when you told him you could 'almost see it'?" she asked.

With the thrill he always felt when talking about his work, he told her about the sculptures he made. He didn't try to explain his plans for the crusher and the driver. He couldn't do it until the image was crystal clear in his mind and transferred to his sketchbook.

Once they'd settled beneath the shade of a sprawling oak with their glasses of lemonade, Luke said, "So, tell me. What's the 'more'?"

Kaydi raised her eyebrows. "More?"

"Earlier, you said there was more to your name."

"Oh, that." Her musical laugh filled the air between them. "Kaydi is only the first half of my first name. The second half is Paris. With a hyphen."

"Your first name is Kaydi hyphen Paris?" he asked.

"Only on official documents. My parents planned on calling me Paris, but that only lasted a week or so. I've been Kaydi or KP ever since."

"Do you have a middle name?"

"Alexandria."

Luke rolled the name around inside his head. *Kaydi-Paris Alexandria.* A unique and unusual name for a unique and unusual woman.

"What's your full name?" she asked.

He almost choked on his lemonade freeze at the unexpected question. Did he dare tell her? "You can't laugh."

"Why would I laugh?"

"Just promise you won't."

"I promise."

"Do you pinkie swear?" He held out his little finger, fully aware that the juvenile gesture was an excuse to touch her again. To see if that first electric shock was a fluke.

"Pinkie swear." Kaydi twisted her little finger around his, and the current surged through him again. Definitely not a fluke.

He let go of her finger and stared into her eyes. "Luke Tecumseh Brannick."

Her cheek muscles relaxed, tightened, and relaxed again as she obviously tried not to smile, but humor sparkled in her eyes.

How much he enjoyed getting lost in the depths of those beautiful brown eyes.

"Tecumseh?" Kaydi asked. "Like the Native American hero?"

"That's right. My grandfather loves history. He chose that name for me, but my parents were wise enough to stick it in the middle."

"Wise indeed. Though I think it's a fine name. A strong name."

"I'm glad you didn't laugh."

"I'm laughing inside." A broad grin rounded her cheeks even more. A moment later, she dissolved into a fit of giggles.

"No fair," Luke teased. "You broke the pinkie swear. Now you must face the consequences."

Kaydi made an obvious effort to pull herself together, but she burst into laughter again. Finally, she took a sip of her lemonade, her gaze never leaving his. "What consequences?" she asked.

"Lunch. With me."

"I kind of already have plans."

Luke's heart sank. "Can you change them?"

"Maybe." Kaydi appeared deep in thought. "I wanted to look around here for a while longer. I was also hoping to talk to one of the estate's owners to find out more about their history."

"The owners are gone, but maybe I could tell you what you want to know. Like I said, I've lived here my whole life. So did my mom before she retired with my stepdad to a life of shuffleboard and bridge in one of those Florida retirement villages."

Luke drew lemonade through his straw and let the refreshing beverage work its magic. He wanted to beg her to go with him, to spend the rest of the day with him, but he didn't want to seem pathetic or desperate. He was neither.

At least he hadn't been until he'd first set eyes on Kaydi.

"Where did you have in mind?" she asked. "For lunch, I mean?"

"There's Aunt Patsy's Porch out by the interstate," Luke answered. "They have the best pie in a hundred miles."

"Anything closer?" Kaydi asked. "I planned to go to the library later this afternoon."

"We've got the usual. Pizza, subs, and a barbecue joint." Where else could he take her? Luke had to come up with something so she wouldn't ditch him. "Do you like Thai food? We have a cool place called Why Thai near the library. Their vegetarian stir-fry is incredible."

"All those sound good to me." Kaydi grinned. "Since I broke the pinkie swear, you decide."

"Nope. You're the tourist and my guest. You choose."

"Barbecue?"

He grinned. "My favorite."

They wandered around the estate sale a little longer. Kaydi asked questions about the home's history and the family who had lived here for at least three generations, and Luke answered them to the best of his ability. She seemed interested in every aspect of the place. Of Magnolia Harbor.

Hopefully, Luke could persuade her to turn that interest to him.

Kaydi

As soon as Kaydi got to the bottom of the inn's broad staircase, she headed toward the kitchen. She hoped Grace or Charlotte would be there instead of mingling with the other guests on the veranda. Kaydi was missing the Sunday evening hospitality hour because she needed to get ready for her date with Luke.

She had to pinch herself to believe she had a date with Luke. From the moment she'd gazed into his dazzling gray eyes, she'd been head over heels in a whirlwind she hadn't seen coming. She meant what she'd told Winnie about waiting for that special person. Who could have imagined that she'd meet him the very next day?

Her purpose for coming to Magnolia Harbor was to find out more about her family's history. Romance had never entered her mind. Okay, maybe it had. But only the tiniest bit as she'd dreamed of her trip and all its wonderful possibilities.

The connection between Kaydi and Luke had been immediate and strong. He'd told her tons of stories about the people who lived in and around Magnolia Harbor, but they'd also talked about other things. About his artwork and her jewelry designs. About their childhoods and college years. About their dreams and philosophies and values.

It was strange how much they had in common for two strangers from vastly different places. He was so charmingly Southern, and she was so Nebraska proud. Yet their hearts seemed to be knitted together. Who could think about past history when the present was so appealing?

She'd never made it to the library. Never made the call to Julep Buckley. Never did any of the investigating she'd planned to do.

Instead, she and Luke had driven separately to the barbecue place and lingered over their lunch until half the afternoon was gone. Then they'd left his motorcycle at the restaurant and taken her rental car to the Magnolia Plantation and Gardens, a huge tourist destination located about an hour northeast of Magnolia Harbor.

This morning, Kaydi had gone to church with Luke, and she'd met a few of the local townspeople. After that, they'd gone to a movie. Now he was taking her to The Tidewater, apparently one of the nicest places in town, for dinner. She didn't remember the last time she'd been this nervous.

Kaydi rapped on the kitchen door and entered. "Anyone here?"

Winston bounded over to her and wagged his tail.

Kaydi smiled as she reached down to scratch behind his ears.

"Come on in." Charlotte stood on the other side of the island wearing an oven mitt and holding a baking pan. "These are crab pinwheels fresh from the oven. Would you like to sample one before I take them out to the veranda?"

The warm aroma tantalized Kaydi's senses and made her mouth water. But how could she eat at a time like this? "They smell delicious, but I'm too nervous."

Charlotte regarded Kaydi's outfit. She wore a forest-green dress with a square neckline, slender straps, and a ruffled hem. "Why do I get the feeling you're not joining us for hospitality hour this evening?"

Kaydi took a deep breath and plunged ahead. "Do you know Luke Brannick?"

Charlotte placed the baking pan on a trivet and focused all her attention on Kaydi. "Sure I do. We have a couple of his sculptures in the gardens."

He had mentioned to Kaydi that Grace and Charlotte had commissioned him for his unique artwork shortly after they opened the inn. "I'd love to see them sometime," she said.

"I can show them to you after I deliver these pinwheels to Grace if you want." Charlotte gave her a knowing smile. "Unless you don't have time because you're going on a date with Luke."

"Yes, I'm going on a date with Luke." Kaydi hopped up and down while letting out a small squeal. "To a place called The Tidewater."

Charlotte beamed. "One of my favorite places."

"Then you can tell me." Kaydi spread her hands to her side and twirled. "Am I dressed appropriately for such a fancy place?"

"You are absolutely gorgeous."

Winston yipped as if in agreement.

Kaydi released a sigh of relief. She ran her hands along the sides of her dress, thankful she had packed it at the last moment. "I wasn't expecting to meet anyone on my trip. Luke wasn't on my agenda, but he's so nice, and I still can't believe he asked me to such an upscale restaurant. I'd have been happy with pizza." She stopped and took a deep breath. "I'm sorry for rambling. But, um, do you mind if I ask what you think of him? I don't suppose you'd want to say anything too bad. Just be honest."

Charlotte seemed to be holding back a severe case of the giggles.

Kaydi couldn't blame her. She'd been more than rambling. She'd been barreling like a runaway freight train on a downward track.

"I don't know Luke that well, but he seems like a great guy," Charlotte answered. "He doesn't date very much, but he volunteers to help out with almost every fundraiser, charity event, parade—you name it, Luke is there. I'd say he's well-liked by everyone."

"That's good to know." Kaydi mused over all that Charlotte had said. "We haven't talked about our former relationships. Though it seems we've talked about everything else since we met. It's been a wonderful weekend, like something from a dream."

"Then dinner at The Tidewater will be the icing on the cake." Charlotte gave a teasing smile. "Unfortunately, their food isn't quite as good as mine."

"Really?"

Charlotte laughed. "Dean Bradley is the owner and chef there. And my boyfriend. We have a friendly rivalry." She shrugged. "Okay, sometimes it's not so friendly. I'm sure whatever you order will be amazing. Just don't tell him I said so."

"I won't," Kaydi promised. She was glad she'd talked to Charlotte. It was nice having a friend she could confide in.

"Are you sure you don't want one of these?" Charlotte gestured toward the pinwheels as she transferred them from the baking pan to a serving platter.

"Maybe just one." Kaydi took a small bite of the hot treat. The crab inside the delicate pinwheel crust was beautifully seasoned, lending a creamy sweetness inside the crisp, buttery pastry. "It's delicious. I knew if I came to the hospitality hour, I'd eat too much and wouldn't want supper." She finished the appetizer, then quickly washed and dried her hands. "Thanks again for your reassurance. I want everything about tonight to be perfect."

"So far, you're nailing it." Charlotte's gaze landed on Kaydi's jeweled butterfly-shaped necklace. "That's an unusual piece you're wearing. Is it vintage?"

"It belonged to my grandmother. She said she designed it, and a talented jeweler made it for her." Kaydi gently tapped the necklace. "When I wear it, I feel like she's here with me, giving me confidence. I suppose that sounds silly."

"No, it doesn't."

"To be honest, I wouldn't be on this trip if it wasn't for her," Kaydi admitted.

"Oh?" Charlotte asked, raising her eyebrows.

Kaydi bit her lip and wished she could take back those words. As nice as Charlotte was, Kaydi wasn't quite ready to tell anyone—not even Luke—the real reason for her visit. This was something she wanted to do on her own. Besides, it was exciting to have a secret when no one knew you had a secret. Like being a detective. Though she hadn't done much detecting. Tomorrow morning she'd have to make up for goofing around all weekend. She'd be disciplined and focused and—

A clock chimed from the other room, startling Kaydi from her musings.

"Luke will be here any minute," Kaydi said. "Are you sure I look okay?"

"Positive." Charlotte placed the baking pan in the sink. "Tell Luke to let Dean know he's there with a special guest from the inn. That I said for him to fix you something extra-special for dessert."

Kaydi clasped her hands. "Oh, you are too kind."

"I want my guests to be pampered," Charlotte said. "Especially one who's on a date with one of our local bachelors."

"I'm so nervous," Kaydi murmured. "My stomach is filled with butterflies."

Charlotte smiled. "Don't you love that feeling?"

Did she?

A bell sounded, signaling someone had entered through the front door of the inn.

"I'll bet that's Luke," Charlotte said.

Kaydi rounded the corner of the island and gave Charlotte a quick hug. "Yes," she said. "I love this feeling."

Kaydi didn't tell Luke what Charlotte had said about dessert, but Charlotte hadn't left anything to chance. After their delicious dinner of baked Dijon salmon sprinkled with pecans and parsley, Dean appeared at their table with a complimentary chocolate-strawberry meringue torte. Kaydi hadn't thought she could eat another bite, but she would have licked the dessert plate clean of all that chocolaty and strawberry goodness if they'd been dining anywhere but The Tidewater.

"That dessert was so good." Kaydi dabbed her lips with the cloth napkin. "I don't think I'll ever be hungry again."

"It was a perfect ending to a perfect dinner," Luke agreed. He was so handsome in gray dress pants and a muted blue button-down shirt.

Kaydi raised her glass. "To a perfect day."

He joined her in the toast, then reached for her hand. "The day isn't over yet. How about a walk down to the dock? It's a wonderful night for a moonlit stroll."

She smiled. "That sounds lovely."

Luke escorted her out of the restaurant and offered his arm.

Kaydi took it, and they sauntered along the boardwalk overlooking the lake. The dark water shimmered beneath the tall overhead lights spaced along the path while the moon's wavering reflection danced among the waves. Other couples were also enjoying an after-dinner stroll. They were probably as reluctant as Kaydi for the evening to end.

She'd been to other fancy restaurants on the arms of young men who were eager to impress her, and a few who seemed to think they were beyond needing to impress, as if they were doing her a favor by asking her out. None of those dates had been as spectacular as this one.

Kaydi appreciated Luke's easygoing confidence, his respect for the waitstaff, and the way his eyes lit up when he introduced her to Dean. All of Luke's fine qualities and more warmed her heart and sent tingles straight down to her toes. Something inexplicable had connected them when they met at the Norwood estate, and the hours they'd spent together since then had only deepened the connection. Strange as it was, Kaydi knew they belonged together.

Luke guided her to a secluded spot along the railing that separated the boardwalk from the sloping bank. "I usually meet a friend for breakfast on Monday mornings at Aunt Patsy's Porch, but I was thinking of standing him up tomorrow."

"You don't think you'll be hungry ever again either?" she teased.

"It's not that." Luke gave her a hopeful smile as he took her hand in both of his. "I'd rather have brunch with you at this little place I know on Hunting Island. It's not far from Hilton Head. What do you say?"

Kaydi wanted to say yes. Spending time with Luke was what she wanted to do more than anything in the world. But she hadn't yet done any of the things she'd planned. No library. No museum. No call to Julep Buckley. Though Luke had started to tell her the history of the area, their conversations tended to veer in other directions. One minute they'd be talking about a Civil War battle that had taken place not far away, and the next they'd start discussing their trips to festivals and flea markets and unusual museums. She didn't know anyone else who was as interested in oddities as Luke. Except for herself.

Nevertheless, Kaydi couldn't let these days slip away without at least making an effort to find out more about her grandmother's family—about her own unknown ancestors. She had to do her research, but she hated to turn him down.

"Don't you have to work tomorrow?" she asked.

"That's a benefit of being my own boss," Luke replied. "I set my hours."

Another incredible connection that knitted them together—an artistic vision that enabled them both to see beyond an object's ordinary appearance to what it could become. Just like her, Luke had resisted the allure of high-paying jobs in more competitive fields and the pressure of well-meaning family and friends to build his own business doing what he loved.

"I could pick you up around nine," he said. "After brunch, we can go up the steps to the top of the Hunting Island Lighthouse. It's the only historic lighthouse in South Carolina that you can still climb. The view of the Atlantic is amazing. That is, if you don't mind the height."

Kaydi minded the height very much, but every fiber of her being shouted *yes*. A gust of wind tugged at her hair, and she tucked the errant strand behind her ear. Her fingers brushed against her grandmother's butterfly necklace. Guilt as heavy as an antique iron pushed into her stomach. "I'd love to go, but I can't. There's something else I need to do."

Luke's disappointed expression tugged at Kaydi's heart, but he managed a smile for her. "Sure. I understand."

"If I spend all my time with you, then I'll never get to the library." Or any of the other places she needed to visit. She should tell him about her plan, but then he'd probably offer to help. She wanted—needed—to do this on her own. To be the smart detective uncovering the clues and solving the mystery. "I've got to do what I came here to do."

"If you don't, then you'll have an excuse to come back again." He grinned. "I wouldn't mind that."

Neither would I. On the other hand, it would take time to save enough money for a future trip, especially if she splurged on another week at the inn. She could always come back and camp out in a tent the entire time.

Yeah, right.

Perhaps if Kaydi arrived at the library as soon as it opened, she could finish her research and still have time to hang out with Luke. "Maybe we could get together for lunch. We could have a picnic, and I'll take care of it."

"How are you going to do that?" he asked.

"I'll ask Charlotte to help me prepare a picnic basket," Kaydi said. "I'm sure you know lots of places that would be great for a picnic. Even the dock at the inn would be fun."

"Tell you what. You bring the food, and I'll pick you up at the dock around noon."

Kaydi furrowed her brows. "What do you mean, you'll pick me up at the dock?"

"We'll picnic on my boat out on the lake." Luke's eyes lit up. "It's the best place I can think of to enjoy good food and good company."

"You have a boat?" she asked.

"Sure do. It actually belongs to my grandfather, but he doesn't have much use for it these days. It's right over there." He pointed toward the marina. "In the summer I probably spend half my leisure time on this lake."

Kaydi stifled a sigh. It had to happen—something they *didn't* have in common. Why did it have to be a boat? She couldn't let him know she preferred keeping both feet on dry land. Besides, it could be an adventure. He was obviously an expert seaman. Or lakeman. Sailor? Tar? Captain? Pirate? She stifled a giggle.

"What's so funny?" Luke asked.

"Do you have a captain's hat?"

"No."

"Not even one of those white caps like Gilligan wore?" she insisted.

"Gilligan from *Gilligan's Island*? No." He drew out the word.

Kaydi smiled. She loved it when his Southern accent, already so charming, deepened even more. Which it always did when he seemed especially amused or excited.

"So, are you going with me on the boat?" Luke asked. "Or are you going to stay holed up in the musty library all day?"

The latter option didn't sound appealing at all. But a boat?

It didn't matter. She couldn't let a day go by without spending time with him.

"You talked me into it," Kaydi said with feigned reluctance. Okay, not totally feigned reluctance. The library opened at nine. Three hours should be plenty of time to find what she needed. Then a half hour to return to the inn and change clothes. "How about we meet at the dock at twelve thirty?"

Luke's smile stretched from ear to ear.

Wow, he was handsome. The more Kaydi got to know him, the more handsome he became. She'd probably go with him to the top of a mountain or the bottom of the sea if he asked her to—and pray she wouldn't be sick on either venture. Why did she have to be afraid of heights and the water? Among other things like spiders and creepy-crawly things and the desert. Yes, the desert would be an awful place to get lost.

Kaydi had done a brave thing coming on this trip all by herself. It was the first time she'd flown alone. First time she'd rented a car by herself. First time she'd planned her very own trip.

She could be brave. She could get on that boat tomorrow. She could think about all the happy things that had happened since her arrival at Magnolia Harbor.

At the top of that list was the guy standing beside her.

"We're going to have a great time," Luke said. "Just wait and see."

She smiled at him, then gazed at the moonlit lake. Yes, they would have a great time.

As long as she kept her nerve.

7

Luke

Whistling a jaunty tune, Luke entered Aunt Patsy's Porch on a cloud-free Monday morning and plopped into the booth opposite his best friend. "Welcome home. How was New York?"

Clint Calloway folded the edition of the *Harbor Gazette* he'd been reading and set it on the table next to his coffee mug. "Business first, then pleasure. Did you find anything worth your while at the Norwood estate sale?"

Luke couldn't hide a grin. "You could say that."

Clint narrowed his eyes as he gave Luke his full attention. "Why do I get the feeling you're not talking about an old rusty doodad you're going to transform into an eye-catching sculpture for the Townsends' yard?"

"Actually, I found two things for the Townsends' sculpture," Luke said. "A sugarcane crusher and an ancient mule-drawn post driver. Once I clean them up, fasten them together, and add the Brannick touch, Blanche and Wesley will have a sculpture that honors their family's agricultural heritage." He paused and took a deep breath. *And I found Kaydi.*

If Clint had been at church yesterday, he would have met Kaydi then. The three of them might have even gone to lunch together. Still, now that Luke was face-to-face with his best friend, it was a little hard to spit out the words. What exactly did a man say when he'd met the only woman who had ever grabbed hold of his heart? Especially when that woman would be flying west again at the end of the week, leaving him as sad and alone as a country-western song?

Clint leaned forward and folded his arms on the table. "What's her name?"

"Is it that obvious?" Luke asked.

"You've got it bad," Clint replied. "Real bad."

"Her name is Kaydi." Luke's grin widened so much his cheeks hurt. "Kaydi-Paris Alexandria Engstrom."

"Say what?" Clint blinked. "Katie-Paris . . . I've already forgotten the rest."

"Kay-DEE, not Ka-TEE," Luke corrected. "She's as amazing as her name is long."

"Where did you meet her?" Clint asked.

"At the Norwood estate sale. She was looking at the sugarcane crusher. Just out of curiosity because she didn't know what it was. So I told her. It's a unique piece. Give me a week or two, and the sculpture will be ready to install. Then you can plan the perfect landscape design to surround it."

Clint shook his head. "You're not going to sidetrack me with business."

"You were the one who said business first," Luke reminded him.

"Forget that," Clint said. "I want to hear more about this gal who has you flying ten feet off the ground."

"What can I say? She's beautiful."

"Of course."

"She's got her own kind of style," Luke continued. "She's confident, like she's going to be who she's going to be no matter what. We talk about everything and nothing. My sides ache from laughing so much, but we can also talk seriously." He shrugged. "I don't know what else to say."

"You've said a lot right there." Clint let out a low whistle. "You've definitely been hooked, my friend."

"No more than you," Luke said. Clint had recently reconnected with his childhood sweetheart, and Luke had never seen his friend happier.

Molly Edwards, the diner's head waitress, appeared at the booth with a carafe of coffee in one hand and a mug for Luke in the other. "Coffee's fresher than milk straight out of the cow. You two fine gentlemen want the usual?" She topped off Clint's cup, then filled Luke's almost to the brim.

"Hold it there, please." Luke held out his hand. "Leave a little room for the creamer."

"You'll ruin good coffee that way," Molly said with a smile. "Now what'll it be this morning?"

"Same as always," Luke and Clint said at the same time.

"You got it." Molly simply wrote the men's names on her order pad. "Scrambled eggs, room on the plate for plenty of ketchup on the side, bacon, and biscuits and gravy for Clint. Two eggs over easy, hash browns, sausage links, and a stack of silver dollar pancakes on the side with blueberry syrup for Luke."

"You should marry me," Luke teased her. "Then I could have that breakfast every morning without coming into the diner."

"I only serve the food. I don't cook it." Molly grinned. "Guess you'll have to keep fending for yourself."

After Molly left, Clint eyed Luke. "Is Kaydi from around here?"

"She lives in Omaha, but she flew here for some kind of personal research project. She's probably already at the library."

"Will I get to meet her before she leaves town?"

"We'll make that happen," Luke promised. "You're going to love her."

Clint shook his head. "I've never seen you like this before."

Though Luke was a few years younger than Clint and the men hadn't been friends when they were growing up in Magnolia Harbor, that had changed when both of them moved back to town after a few years away for college and work. Clint often commissioned Luke to create sculptures for the landscape designs he created for his clients. He had also helped Luke with his own landscape design when he moved into the gatehouse on his family estate.

Luke leaned back. "I've never met anyone like her."

"Anyone like who?" Molly asked as she appeared with their orders.

Luke's ears warmed. Talking to Clint about Kaydi was one thing, but he didn't want to talk about her to Molly. It probably didn't matter. He'd already started the gossip train rolling when he took Kaydi to church yesterday. Several people who usually didn't seek him out were eager to meet the lovely young woman at his side.

"Leave him alone." Clint aimed a disarming smile at Molly. "He needs more time to make a good impression on the lady before we start telling her about all his flaws and failings."

"Luke doesn't have any flaws or failings." Molly playfully slapped Clint's shoulder. "Neither do you. I'd say you're two of the most handsome young fellas in Magnolia Harbor. I could tell your lady all kinds of good things, Luke. Bring her by during my shift and just see if I don't."

Luke laughed. "I knew I could count on you."

"Of course you can. Now both of you eat up before your eggs get cold." She left them, muttering something about Luke's lady being a lucky gal.

"Thanks." Luke sprinkled pepper on his eggs. "You distracted her nicely."

"Easy to do," Clint replied. "You know she's always thought of you like a son."

Luke harrumphed. "Both of us."

"I do appreciate the way she takes care of us." Clint dragged a forkful of his scrambled eggs through a pool of ketchup.

"Do you think you could get together for lunch one day this week?" Luke took a sip of coffee.

"What about today?" Clint asked. "No time like the present."

"Already have plans." Luke smiled. "We're going out on my boat for a picnic. No offense, but you're not invited."

"None taken," Clint said. "Don't you have an appointment to meet with Pastor Glen and Penny this afternoon? They're eager to see your ideas for a kid-friendly sculpture."

Glen Abrams, the minister of Fellowship Christian Church, a compassionate soul in a wiry body with white Einstein hair, had given his wife, Penny, a gift certificate for Clint's landscape design services for Valentine's Day. It had been the ideal present for Penny, who was eager to make a few changes to her backyard but was overwhelmed with the possibilities. Clint had helped her make choices, and she'd implemented several of his suggestions.

The final touch would be one of Luke's original sculptures that the grandchildren could climb around on without getting hurt.

"I talked to Penny first thing this morning." Luke topped his pancake stack with pats of butter. "I'm headed there next."

"Mind if I tag along?" Clint asked. "We can talk about a few planting options at the same time."

"Might as well," Luke said. "I already did a few sketches last night."

"Couldn't sleep, huh?"

"What makes you think that?"

"I've been there," Clint said as he squeezed more ketchup onto his plate.

"So how was New York?" Luke asked.

"Big and noisy. Somehow it was a lot of fun in spite of all that."

As they ate their breakfast, Clint told Luke about his visit to the Big Apple to see his fiancée, Presley Ingram, a former fashion designer. Presley's grandparents had owned the inn before Grace and Charlotte bought it. Clint and Presley, who had been each other's first love, had reunited last Valentine's Day and were now working out the complexities of a long-distance relationship, their upcoming wedding, and the details of Presley's move to Magnolia Harbor.

At the time of their reunion, Luke had been happy for his friend—Clint and Presley were perfect for each other—but also a little jealous. Luke had prayed for a long time to find the woman who was right for him.

Maybe God had finally answered that prayer by bringing Kaydi-Paris Alexandria Engstrom to town.

Thank You, God, Luke prayed as he poured syrup over his pancakes. *And please let me be the right man, the perfect man, for her.*

8

Grace

Winston's brown eyes held so much sadness that Grace finally gave in. "You can come with me, but stay away from any skunks."

Immediately the little guy's ears perked up, and his tail, which had been coiled about his back legs, wagged furiously.

"How is it you know exactly what I'm saying?" She reached down to pat his head. "Come on then. Remember what I said—no skunks."

Grace wasn't sure if it was her imagination or if the fragrance of eau de skunk still clung in the air around the dog. After using the solution Clayton had suggested and other shampoos, Winston finally seemed to be free of the awful odor. Winnie had given him the all clear, and none of the guests who'd made friends with the well-mannered shih tzu mix had complained.

Grace shuddered. Hopefully they wouldn't have a repeat of that situation, but if they did, she was ready. A bottle of the de-skunking solution sat between his shampoo and the basket holding his grooming tools on the shelf in the laundry room designated for all things Winston.

As they neared the grandfather stump, the name given to what remained of the giant live oak that had been struck by lightning several years ago, Winston gave a couple of cheerful barks and ran ahead.

"I hope that wasn't a skunk bark," Grace muttered and trotted after him.

The sound of rustling drew her attention to the trio of slender pines christened by the former owners of the mansion as the three sisters. A man slipped through the trees and out of sight. Who could that have been?

Winston barked again, and Grace hurried after him. When she reached the clearing surrounding the stump, she stopped. Danielle sat on one of the slatted benches cuddling Winston in her lap. Her face was buried in his fur.

She glanced up, her eyes rimmed in red, as Grace approached.

"Are you all right?" Grace asked.

Danielle swiped at her eyes, then buried her hands in Winston's silky coat as if seeking solace in his presence.

Grace understood that feeling. How often in recent weeks had Winston's soothing presence, whether it was his weight in her lap or his tongue against her skin, given her strength? Or at least helped her to stay centered when the world around her seemed to be out of control?

Grace took a seat beside her guest. "I don't want to pry, but if you need to talk to someone, I'm here." She peered beyond the three sisters. "I saw someone leaving. Who was it?"

Danielle startled. "This is a lovely spot for being alone," she said, changing the subject.

"I think so too," Grace said. Obviously Danielle wasn't going to answer her question. *How can I help her, Father? Please give me the right words to say.*

Silence. Perhaps that was what Danielle needed most. Plus, a bit of love from Winston who had settled contentedly in her lap.

"You've made a nice life for yourself," Danielle remarked. "It seems so peaceful."

"I do love it here." Grace relaxed her shoulders and gazed at the plot of wildflowers growing nearby. The riotous colors and various textures brightened this out-of-the way corner of the property. Maybe later, she'd return and cut a few of the blossoms to create a bouquet for Charlotte.

Right now, though, she wanted to do whatever it took to help Danielle. Perhaps if Grace didn't appear tense, Danielle would feel more at ease. Maybe she'd even open up about her troubles. Especially if Grace gave her a gentle nudge. "It's not always so quiet. We've had a few strange experiences."

"Like what?" Danielle asked. She appeared interested, and maybe she was. On the other hand, she probably wanted to distract Grace—to get her talking so she didn't have to.

"Once we had a woman come here for her honeymoon. Alone."

"You're kidding."

"I'm not." Grace chuckled at the disbelief on Danielle's face. "Thankfully, it all ended well. Her fiancé showed up, and love prevailed."

Danielle lowered her gaze. "It's nice to know that sometimes it does."

Is Danielle here to heal a broken heart? Grace let the idea roll around in her head. Anything was possible. Perhaps that was why she'd taken a taxi. She didn't want the person who had hurt her to track her down. Or perhaps she'd been the one who'd hurt someone else.

Though that didn't explain why she was here at the grandfather stump with a strange man. Probably the same man Winnie had seen her with at the bookstore.

"Do you miss it?" Danielle asked. "The corner office? The client meetings? The creative voices?"

"No." Even Grace was surprised by how adamantly she answered Danielle's question. She took a moment to consider her quick response. "The perks and sense of accomplishment of creating a winning campaign were fulfilling, but the ebb and flow of my life is so different now. It's rewarding in a more meaningful way."

"I used to think I could never give it up," Danielle said. "Lately,

I've realized my mind was always on the next rung in the ladder. Too often I thought that once I reached that one, I'd be fulfilled and happy. But that's not true. With each climb, the hours just get longer and the expectations even higher."

So maybe it was career burnout that had brought Danielle to Magnolia Harbor.

"It's a stressful job. Though I'm sure you do it very well." Grace shook her head. "I hope that didn't sound patronizing. I truly meant it. You're talented and creative and a hard worker."

"I've enjoyed the challenges, though sometimes I wonder . . ." Danielle's voice faded.

Grace didn't rush to fill the silence. If Danielle wanted to confide in her, then she could do so. Grace wouldn't pressure her to share anything.

"I'm glad you're happy." Danielle lifted Winston as she stood, gave him a hug, and placed him on the bench beside Grace. "Hold on to what you have here."

Grace stared after Danielle as she walked away. Her thoughts were in a whirl as she tried to reconcile the professional, in-charge Danielle from Maddox Creative with the hurting woman who had been sitting beside her.

I don't think I helped her at all, Lord.

Winston curled beside her and rested his nose on her leg.

She absentmindedly stroked his fur. *What can I do for her?*

The answer seemed to be right beside her. Like Winston, she could be a quiet presence, always there to provide comfort when needed. It was up to Danielle, not Grace, to decide when those moments occurred.

In the meantime, Grace could only pray for Danielle and remember that they weren't rivals or colleagues anymore.

With a shock, she realized that she knew very little about the *real* Danielle Holloway.

Kaydi

The trip to the Heritage Library had not been the fascinating adventure Kaydi had imagined it would be. Phyllis Gendel, the head librarian, was out of town at a conference, and the librarian on duty had only lived in the area a couple of years. She was as helpful as she could be by pointing out the section of books on the history of Magnolia Harbor and demonstrating how to use the computerized genealogical database.

Kaydi entered *Callie Jo Emmett*, her grandma's maiden name, into the computer search bar and received zero results. She also entered *Joseph Piper*, her grandfather's name. The names of his parents appeared, but Kaydi already knew those. On the old census records she'd located prior to her trip, her great-grandfather's occupation was listed as a gardener. The name of his employer wasn't included in the scant information.

For the next hour, Kaydi flipped through the pages of the most likely books on Magnolia Harbor history and scanned the indexes for any Emmetts or Pipers.

She didn't discover any information about either family.

Discouraged but not defeated, Kaydi called Julep Buckley's number. The phone rang several times before going to voice mail.

Kaydi took a deep breath and left her name and phone number. "I'm staying at the Magnolia Harbor Inn," she added. "I'm here to find out anything I can about my family. I'd love to talk to you. That is, if you don't mind returning my call."

She disconnected. Now what should she do?

Kaydi thanked the librarian for her assistance. When she mentioned she hadn't uncovered any useful information, the librarian suggested she visit the *Harbor Gazette*, one of the town's two newspapers.

Kaydi thanked her again and went to the newspaper office, where a staff member set her up at an old microfiche machine.

Before arriving in Magnolia Harbor, Kaydi had envisioned scouring through old dusty books and archives and making the discovery she longed to make—the proof that her grandmother was the outcast daughter of one of Magnolia Harbor's most prominent families. The reality of skimming through pages and microfiche film wasn't nearly as romantic or exciting as she'd imagined.

If only her grandmother had been able to share more of her history before she died. That had been impossible when her memories seemed to come and go. The stories she'd told had been new to everyone, and only Kaydi believed them. Everyone else in the family thought her grandma was delusional. All her talk of balls and dances, of shopping trips to Atlanta and vacations in Savannah hadn't seemed likely.

Her grandfather had worked as a school custodian until his death several years ago from a sudden heart attack. Her grandmother had helped support their small family by taking in ironing, and later by utilizing her sewing skills to make alterations for a local bridal shop. She'd retired long ago and remained in her modest home until her dementia made it unsafe for her to be alone.

To Kaydi, her grandmother's reminiscences had rung true. It was odd that her grandma had never mentioned the parties or the trips to anyone in the family before her mind began to slip away. But she'd always been guarded about her past, leading the family to speculate that she was hiding an awful secret. They used to joke about the possibilities, but they never believed their own suppositions.

"Better not to know," Kaydi's mom had remarked more than once.

Kaydi couldn't imagine that her grandmother had ever been involved in anything nefarious. She was the kindest person Kaydi had ever met. She would have never done anything criminal or horrible. Plus, Kaydi had the added benefit of being her grandma's undisputed favorite. Kaydi knew she heard even more stories from her grandmother than her mother or her uncle had. She had surmised that her grandmother's reason for keeping her past a secret was because of a romance.

Perhaps a forbidden romance. After all, when the daughter of a grand house eloped with the gardener's son, surely the resulting scandal would be horrendous.

Though her grandmother had never said that she had eloped, Kaydi was certain that was what had happened. Now she was determined to find her grandmother's family, talk to any living relatives, and see what she could learn of her grandparents' starry-eyed romance. Had the family ever forgiven their daughter? Had they tried to find her after she ran away?

It was the real-life story of a love often found only in novels and movies. A mystery that waited to be solved. Kaydi was determined to be the one to do just that. She'd locate her grandmother's family—her family—and the two branches would be united again. How amazing would that be?

All her determination and zeal that had seemed so important before she left home was now face-to-face with the mundane and boring task of research. Not exciting research either, but the kind of tedious research that strained her eyes, made her shoulders ache, and gave her a sore back. She peered at slide after slide of microfiche but discovered nothing of interest.

Kaydi had to admit that the old news stories were sometimes humorous. The paper was filled with little items about who had eaten dinner with whom and what they'd been wearing and who had company from out of town—all the society news that filled today's social media feeds. Yet none of those society items mentioned Callie Jo Emmett or Joseph Piper.

It was as if her grandparents had never existed.

Magnolia Harbor was the name that her grandmother had whispered over and over again in her more lucid moments. She'd pleaded for Kaydi to go there, find Carrie Ann, and tell her how sorry she was, but she never mentioned to Kaydi what she was sorry about. Who was Carrie Ann anyway?

All this eyestrain was getting her nowhere except to Frustrationville. Meanwhile, Luke would soon be waiting for her to join him at the dock.

She couldn't wait to see him. She could wait forever to get on that boat.

She couldn't wait for the minutes to pass by. She wanted them to drag.

Finally, Kaydi sat back in the uncomfortable chair and raised her arms toward the ceiling. "What am I supposed to do?" she whispered.

She'd been sent on a heroine's quest only to be distracted by a knight in shining armor on a motorcycle. She'd tried to finish her task, but she'd been slain by the dragon named Boredom. Could she rise up and complete her task?

Of course she could. But not without a dose of the magic elixir, Luke's smile, which could only be found near the dock at the Magnolia Harbor Inn.

Entertained by her own musings, Kaydi shut down the machine and returned the films to their proper places. Tomorrow was another day and all that. A new day, and perhaps the day she'd figure out her grandmother's cryptic clues. She decided to call Julep again in the morning.

For now, the heroine had a date with her knight.

10

Danielle

After leaving Grace and Winston near the tree stump, Danielle returned to the inn. She and Ace needed to finish their conversation soon.

Danielle sent him a text, asking him to suggest a location away from the inn. They agreed on a time and a place, and Danielle took the shuttle into town to rent a car. She drove from the rental car agency to the rendezvous point and found refuge from the sweltering June sun on a cement bench under a sprawling shade tree with Spanish moss hanging from its branches.

Here, at the Shady Rest Cemetery in nearby Snellville, perhaps she and Ace would have the privacy they desperately needed. How unfortunate that earlier in the day Grace decided to visit the out-of-the-way garden at the very moment when Danielle needed total seclusion.

Ace shouldn't have taken off the way he did. Danielle realized he was terrified. She remained convinced they needed to confide in someone. The two of them weren't going to solve anything on their own, and neither of them could keep hiding out forever.

She took a deep breath and gazed around this section of the cemetery. The stones were weathered, and the monuments had an old-fashioned look about them. They were much different from the markers and obelisks closer to the entrance, which seemed to have a more modern sensibility.

She was thankful that the place was quiet. The peacefulness seemed to enter Danielle's spirit and give her a tranquility she sorely needed.

At the sound of tires on the gravel drive, she turned toward the lane that wound through the grassy sections. A truck bearing a company logo traveled at a snail's pace. She stepped out from the shelter of the tree and waved.

Ace waved in response. It didn't take him long to wind his way closer to their rendezvous point and step out of the truck.

He walked toward her and leaned against the tree, then put his hands into the pockets of his cargo shorts. A pair of work gloves stuck out of the back pocket. Despite the heat, he wore thick socks with work boots, the typical uniform for his temporary profession.

"After the way I left you, I wasn't sure I'd hear from you again," he said quietly. "When I saw Grace headed our way, I ran. I can't face her. I can't face anyone."

Her heart ached at the need beneath his words. A catastrophe had brought them together, but what about when it was over? Danielle was trying not to care about him as anything more than a colleague who'd gotten entangled in a mess he couldn't get out of. The more time they spent together, the more she grew to know him as a person instead of her accomplice in this surreal disaster, and the more she liked him. The more she wanted to know him.

Sometimes she'd catch him watching her with something akin to hope in his eyes. Perhaps she was mistaken, but she didn't think so. He was attracted to her too. How could either of them consider a potential romance with this horrendous mess hanging over their heads?

"I don't blame you for leaving," Danielle said, her voice quiet.

"Did you tell Grace?" Ace asked.

"No." She peered up at him and waited for him to meet her gaze. "I still think we should."

He slid down the trunk of the tree until he sat on the ground, his forearms resting on his drawn-up knees. "I don't know what she could do. What if she tells Maddox Creative where you are?"

"She wouldn't do that."

"How can you be sure?" Ace persisted.

He was right. Danielle couldn't be sure. It wasn't as if she and Grace had been the best of friends when they worked together. And then there had been that incident with Grace's protégé, the backstabbing schemer Grace had groomed to take her place as vice president. Danielle was positive that Grace hadn't been pleased that she had received the promotion instead.

Still, Grace had been nothing but friendly and kind since Danielle's arrival at the inn. She was obviously curious about the reason for Danielle's stay, but so far, she hadn't crossed the line into prying. Instead, she seemed to be waiting for Danielle to open up.

"You don't know how many times I've wished I could go back to that day," he said. "I thought I was doing the right thing, and then it all fell apart."

Danielle didn't say anything. She already knew the story. But when Ace felt the need to talk, she always listened. It was the only way she could show her support for him. Besides, she was in almost as deep as he was.

"If only I'd been more careful," Ace continued. "If I'd had a different way of getting that information."

"You did the right thing," Danielle assured him. "It's the chief financial officer who's in the wrong. Not you."

"Yet he's still showing up for work each day while I'm on the lam." He shook his head. "All because of a simple sweepstakes."

"There's no such thing as a simple sweepstakes." She'd handled enough promotional contests to know that glitches sometimes happened, but there were certain protocols and guidelines in place to prevent actual fraud and cheating. Unfortunately, those protocols didn't always work. "The company president should be glad you found out about the theft of the winning pieces before the contest began."

"Unless he's in on it too."

Danielle knew that it was a good possibility. The medium-size restaurant chain where Ace worked as an accountant had begun as a family restaurant. Now they had multiple locations throughout the southeastern states and a few closer to the Mississippi River.

From what Ace had told her, many of the corporate heads were either related to one another or were childhood friends of the original owners. Nepotism was common when it came to promotions. Ace had shared his frustration that he seemed to have risen as far in the company as he'd ever get. That frustration, expressed to his superiors when he'd last been passed over, could now come back to haunt him.

"They'll say I did it." Ace blew out a deep breath. "They'll claim I bribed someone at Maddox to give me the winning pieces."

"If only we knew if someone actually did that." If someone had, who could it have been? A member of the restaurant's marketing team who worked as a liaison with Maddox Creative on special projects? A security guard entrusted with the integrity of the contest as he transported the game pieces from one location to another?

"They'll think I bribed you," Ace said. "Especially since you've disappeared too."

A shiver of fear zipped along Danielle's spine. Another fear she already knew all too well. Running away made them both look guilty. Plus, whoever was behind the theft had been furious to find his—or her—plans had been thwarted.

The sweepstakes had been canceled quickly and quietly. Neither the restaurant's board of directors nor the advertising firm had wanted the public to get even a whiff of a potential scandal. Scapegoats were needed, and the finger-pointing had started immediately. For reasons she didn't understand, a few of those fingers had been pointed at her.

She'd been the one to bring the restaurant chain on board. Her team had helped the restaurant's sweepstakes committee—made up of executives from their legal, marketing, and accounting departments—stay within federal and state guidelines as they worked together to design the sweepstakes.

"We need a go-between," Danielle said. "Someone who can return the files you took by mistake."

"They'll still charge me with theft," Ace reasoned. "They're already trying to pin the sweepstakes scandal on me. You know they are."

She slowly nodded. They'd had this discussion again and again. When Ace, who represented the accounting department on the sweepstakes committee, had suspected the chief financial officer planned to frame him for the sweepstakes debacle, he'd searched through the accounting files and located several expenditures that didn't make sense. As he downloaded those files, he'd inadvertently copied proprietary information.

Almost all businesses were concerned with the adverse effects of corporate espionage. Even though Ace hadn't intentionally taken the protected documents, he could be imprisoned for accessing the information. Never mind that the financial records could lead to the real culprits in the theft of the winning sweepstakes tickets.

To deflect any possible repercussions, the restaurant chain hoped to place the lion's share of the blame onto Maddox Creative's massive shoulders. Even though Danielle had done nothing wrong, she could sense the suspicion swirling around her from the other high-level executives, especially after they learned she and Ace had gone to dinner a couple of times.

Her head spun as she considered the trouble they were in and how quickly their routine lives had been turned upside down by events out of their control.

"What are we going to do?" Danielle asked. "We can't hide forever."

"Why not?" His smile was broad and teasing, but the sadness in his eyes belied his carefree attitude. "We could go somewhere far away. Montana or even Canada."

Danielle returned his smile. Even if he didn't feel as lighthearted as he acted, she wanted to encourage him and do her best to help him feel better. Besides, she liked the way he said "we," as if they were partners. Or perhaps something more. What did it hurt to play along with the fantasy? "A cabin in the wilds of Montana. That sounds amazing."

"Do you know how to ride a horse?" Ace asked.

"No, but I've always wanted to learn."

"Do you know how to brand a calf?"

"I'm afraid not."

"Me either. I guess that rules out ranching." Ace shrugged. "Probably just as well. I don't think I'm cut out to raise horses or cattle."

"All I know is marketing." It was a field Danielle had loved since high school when she'd taken an elective class on marketing and public relation strategies. Her college classes had been a breeze, and her corporate career had been stellar. Until now.

Ace released a heavy sigh. "All I know how to do is crunch numbers."

A silence descended upon them as the impossible dream of a Montana cabin faded into the harsh light of reality.

After a few moments, Ace stood and joined Danielle on the bench. She scooted over to make room for him.

"We're going to get through this," he said. "I know we will."

"We will." She put as much enthusiasm into her voice as she could, but she didn't see how they could emerge unscathed. Her reputation would be stained even if she was exonerated. Whatever happened, she'd need to reevaluate her role at Maddox Creative. If she still had a job there when this was over.

"Maybe I could start my own marketing firm." Danielle bit her lip. She hadn't meant to say the thought out loud.

Ace slowly nodded. "Any chance you'll need an accountant?"

"I believe I will." Suddenly her heart seemed lighter than it had in days. "Do you know of anyone who might be available?"

"I know a very competent and capable accountant who would be perfect for your company." He frowned. "Unless he's in jail."

"You're not going to jail," she assured him. "I won't let that happen."

"You may not be able to stop it." He shifted in his seat and took her hand between both of his. "If that happens, don't try to defend me. You need to protect yourself."

"I'll be fine." Danielle intertwined her fingers with his and rested her head on his shoulder. "We're both going to be fine."

"I hope you're right."

For a long while they sat on the bench as the shade from the huge moss-covered tree shifted with the lowering of the sun. They'd accomplished nothing. They still had no plan.

But for this moment in time, they could rest in the comfort of a true and trusting friendship, and that was no small thing.

11

Luke

The day couldn't be more perfect for motoring around the lake. White clouds accented the blue sky, trailing slender wisps as they moved at a snail's pace across the sky. The sun, bright and hot, tossed sun pennies onto the crests of the waves that lapped against the sides of the pontoon boat.

The only thing not perfect was the tension in Kaydi's shoulders as she sat in the corner of the bench seat, arms wrapped around her knees, which were drawn to her chest.

Once they were in the middle of the lake, Luke cut the motor and swiveled in the nearby pilot's chair.

Kaydi glanced at him.

Before she turned toward the distant shore, Luke caught a glimpse of her expression. She appeared sick, then embarrassed. "I'm going to lower the anchor," he announced.

She nodded, and her shoulders hunched even more.

Instead of going to the bow to take care of the anchor, Luke moved to the bench. He longed to pull her into his arms. Or simply take her hand. Especially if either gesture would bring a touch of color to her pale cheeks and make the fear in her eyes go away. No, it was too soon.

Wasn't it?

They'd known each other only a couple of days. Though, in a strange way, he felt like they'd known each other all their lives.

He settled for a light tap on her forearm. "Or we could return to shore and have our picnic on one of the docks."

"I'm okay." She met his gaze, and this time her smile appeared genuine and a little apologetic. "I want to be okay."

"You could have told me you were a landlubber," he teased. "Or didn't you know?"

"Unfortunately, I knew." Kaydi blew out a long breath. "But I'm determined not to spoil our plans." She loosened the death grip around her legs and shifted to place her bare feet on the floor of the boat. Her shoulders relaxed, but she gripped the edge of the bench cushion.

Wow, she was beautiful. Everything about her—from the silkiness of her highlighted hair with its angular style to the curve of her cheeks, the light dusting of freckles, and her deep-brown eyes—stirred something within him that he'd never felt before.

Though that wasn't quite true. Luke had been in the shadows of such an attraction before—the one that held his parents within its warm and loving embrace. For the first time, as if he were seeing with new eyes, he admitted that this was what he'd been waiting for all his life. Why the few relationships he'd had before now had always felt like something was missing.

Something *was* missing.

This.

This indefinable, inexplicable tug.

He followed Kaydi's gaze to the calm, sun-drenched waves that cradled the gently rocking boat. Her tender smile and her effort to be brave pulled Luke closer to her. He rested his arm on the bench back behind her.

"It's beautiful out here," she murmured. "Too beautiful to miss for any reason."

"My mom used to get seasick, but that never stopped her." Memories washed over him of the many summer days his family had spent on this lake together. Oftentimes just the three of them. Sometimes with his grandfather or a few close friends.

He'd been blessed with an idyllic childhood and loving parents. He wanted to share this joy with Kaydi. "If Dad was going out on the boat, Mom was determined to be right out there with him. They were practically inseparable."

Luke pursed his lips as an unexpected tidal wave of grief washed over him, more powerful than he'd experienced in years. "Until he died."

Kaydi laced her fingers with his and leaned into him.

His pulse raced, yet her touch was as natural, as comforting, as if they'd always been together.

"What happened?" she asked.

"A heart attack. He was only forty-six, but he had a stressful job. He worked eighty to ninety hours a week. I suppose that's why he devoted all his free time to us. To make up for the late nights and missed ball games." Wonderful memories surfaced in Luke's mind. His parents dancing in the kitchen. Fishing expeditions in the Atlantic. Season tickets to the Clemson University football games. A too-good-to-be-true family, his grandpa had always said. Until his dad left them.

"Forty-six is so young. I'm sorry."

"It was hard," he admitted. He didn't want the gloom of mourning to cast a shadow over their time together. Kaydi wouldn't be in Magnolia Harbor much longer. He wanted to make sure her memories of her time here were happy ones. So happy she'd want to return. Maybe even stay.

Now he was getting ahead of himself.

Or was he?

He mentally tucked the thought to the back of his mind. Something to wonder about later. "Eventually Mom remarried and got over her seasickness. She and my stepfather cruise the St. Johns River all the time. They love the Florida life."

Kaydi's free hand pressed against her stomach. "I'd like to know her secret."

Luke scrunched his eyes as another memory floated within reach. "She used to suck on Life Savers. Butter rum was the only flavor that worked."

"Butter rum Life Savers?" Kaydi asked. Her fingers stiffened against his. "Are you sure?"

"Positive. Why?"

She let go of his hand, then reached for her bag and rummaged through its contents. She held up a pack of Life Savers. "Winnie Bennett gave these to me the first night I was here. I didn't want to take them, but she insisted. Almost as if she somehow knew I'd need them."

Luke laughed softly. "Winnie is a treasure. She does seem to have a knack for giving the right gift to the right person at the right time."

"I'm so glad." Kaydi unwrapped the roll and popped a Life Saver into her mouth. "These are delicious. Want one?"

"Why not?" Luke took one of the candies. "Do you want to go back to the dock?"

"Not yet. Let's give these a chance."

"Then I'd better tend to that anchor." He reluctantly left her side and strode to the bow. Under his guidance, the anchor descended into the lake's depths. He glanced at Kaydi as the chains rattled their way downward.

Kaydi waved the packet at him. "These are really good." She put another one into her mouth. Her cheeks no longer seemed as pale, and her eyes sparkled.

"Do you think you could eat something?" Luke asked.

"I'm suddenly starving," Kaydi said, sounding surprised. "Shall we see what Charlotte prepared for us?"

"Absolutely." He dragged the basket from its place beneath one of the benches and set it on the table.

Kaydi joined him. All signs of her earlier distress seemed to have vanished.

Together they unpacked the delicacies Charlotte had made. They found deli meats and cheeses, freshly baked hoagie rolls, raw veggies, chimichurri potato salad, seedless grapes, and lemon-blueberry bars. Bottles of water, a thermos of sweet tea, and assorted condiments were also in the basket.

Once they had prepared their sandwiches and filled their plates, they returned to the bench.

Luke grinned at Kaydi. "I'm glad those Life Savers worked."

"Me too," she said. "Otherwise I wouldn't have been able to enjoy such a wonderful picnic."

"It's funny," Luke said. "The little things you forget. Like those Life Savers. I haven't thought about those in years. I guess I don't talk about my parents very often. It's been nice talking about them today."

"I like hearing about your family." Kaydi poured sweet tea from the thermos into two glasses and gave one to Luke. "It sounds like you had a happy childhood."

"I did. That was something I took for granted at the time. I didn't realize how uncommon it was until I grew up."

"I know what you mean. Same here." Kaydi waved a carrot stick as she talked. "I mean, a few of my friends had parents who were divorced. My parents had something between them that was very special. A lot of love." Her cheeks flushed after she said the word, and she hurriedly chomped on the carrot.

Was it possible to love someone you'd met only a couple of days before? It seemed unlikely. And yet . . .

Luke tucked those thoughts away too. How could he hope to be objective when this beautiful woman turned his senses into mush?

Fortunately, she changed the subject. "So how did you end up as a sculptor?"

"I tried to do the corporate thing for a while," he answered. "Worked the long hours. Sat in a cubicle."

She wrinkled her nose. "How did you stand it?"

"Not very well." Luke bit into his sandwich, recalling those days when he was mired in his entry-level position at a large insurance company. "I guess in some way I wanted to try to restore the family fortune, but that's never going to happen. It's why Dad worked so hard and why he died so young. It took more years than it should have for me to realize I was trying to live his dream instead of my own."

"What's your dream?" Kaydi asked.

Luke shrugged. In one way, he felt like he could tell Kaydi anything and everything, but what if she thought he'd given up on a promising career too soon? That he wasn't living up to his full potential?

Most people in Magnolia Harbor seemed to like him, but he'd heard the whispers. Some people believed he should be doing more with his life than wasting his time on art projects. But he didn't want to end up like his dad—spending most of his days trapped behind his desk only to die too young.

Luke had gradually come to terms with how some people thought of him. He'd learned to ignore the whispers. To gain confidence in his choice to live the kind of life he wanted to live.

A creative life. A giving life. A fulfilling life.

Kaydi seemed like a free spirit herself, and she was also dedicated to living a creative life. But that didn't mean she didn't want stability from a potential partner.

He chided himself for rushing things.

Except he wasn't. His heart was already so tangled up inside. Sure, they needed more time together. Though he was already positive that more time wouldn't change how he felt about her.

Would Kaydi's view of him change if she knew he came from one of the town's founding families? That their estate was now a run-down mansion—the glory days a thing of the distant past that would never be restored? Would she understand his choices then?

"To live a simple life." The admission, spoken out loud, surprised him. "That's my dream."

She tilted her head, her clear eyes holding his gaze.

For a moment, he was afraid she wasn't going to speak.

Then she smiled and said, "The best kind."

Good thing he was holding his plate on his lap, or Luke would have grabbed her and kissed her right then and there. Instead, he took another bite of his sandwich. And said a silent prayer for both of their hearts.

Grace

The serving table at Monday evening's hospitality hour, laden with fish tacos and other mouthwatering appetizers, was also a feast for the eyes. Bright-red apples, polished to a shine, graced a colorful fruit salad. Crackers and cheeses were artistically arranged on a wooden board. A silver carousel held miniature cupcakes that the Zema family had helped to bake and decorate.

Grace smiled with satisfaction at Charlotte's uncanny ability to display her dishes as if preparing them for a photo session. She handed plates to Kaydi and Luke.

"Thanks again for inviting me to stay," Luke said. "This definitely beats leftovers. Or another lonely take-out supper."

Lonely? Grace suspected Luke exaggerated when it came to his lack of plans for supper. She sneaked a peek at Kaydi, who only seemed to have eyes for Luke.

"We're glad to have you with us." Grace had been at the dock when Luke and Kaydi returned from their boat ride. Extending the invitation for Luke to join them had been the hospitable thing to do, and it had certainly broadened the smiles on both their faces.

Young love.

She pushed the thought away. "The weather was wonderful for being out on the water."

"It was," Luke agreed, "but I'm not sure Kaydi liked it very much."

"I liked it," Kaydi protested. She faced Grace. "Though I got a little seasick at first."

"A little?" Luke echoed. "You were leaning over the side of the boat so far that I was afraid you were going to fall in the water. I shouted at the fish to get out of the way before something terrible happened."

"That's not true at all." Kaydi laughed. The young woman had a good sense of humor to put up with Luke's teasing. "You'd better watch out, or I'll push you overboard next time we go boating."

"You heard her," Luke said to Grace. "She agreed to go boating again."

"I heard her," Grace said, "but I wouldn't hold her to it."

"Me either." Luke tapped Kaydi's elbow with his. "Though today is a day I'll never forget."

"Neither will I." Kaydi's cheeks flushed. "I promise I'll go boating with you again."

"Do you promise not to throw me overboard?" Luke joked.

"We'll have to wait and see about that," Kaydi replied.

"What if I promise you a lifetime's supply of butter rum Life Savers?" he asked.

Luke and Kaydi made their selections, then wandered to the other end of the veranda to enjoy their appetizers at a table set for two.

Charlotte appeared next to Grace with a dish of avocado halves filled with a tangy seafood salad. "If I hadn't seen it with my own eyes, I wouldn't have believed it. Luke is positively smitten."

"It is amazing, isn't it?" Grace poured herself a glass of white wine. "I think Kaydi feels the same way."

"There's nothing quite like young love." Charlotte gave a little laugh. "But I'm rather fond of thirtysomething love too." She regarded the table. "Oh no, I forgot the serving spatula for these tapas. I'll be right back."

Charlotte's words reverberated in Grace's mind despite her efforts to squash them. *There's nothing quite like young love.*

Grace had said something similar to Spencer the day after their Valentine's Day dinner. What a lovely night that had been. At Spencer's request, Winnie and The Busy Bees had prepared a surprise dinner for Grace. Afterward, Grace and Spencer had walked from the barn, where the dinner had been served in a specially decorated nook, to the dock in the moonlight.

The next morning, Grace and Spencer were leaving to spend the day in Charleston when they saw Clint Calloway and Presley Ingram. The Busy Bees had brought them together with a surprise Valentine's Day dinner too.

"Young love is so sweet," Grace had said.

"Grown-up love is too," Spencer had whispered right before he kissed her.

All that had happened before Hank had returned and flipped Grace's world upside down.

As she quickly blinked to get rid of any tears that might dare to fall, she glanced at Kaydi and Luke. They were talking and laughing as if they'd known each other all their lives instead of a couple of days. What would happen to their budding relationship when Kaydi went home?

Chet and Mandy and their sons walked onto the veranda, and Grace spent a few minutes describing the hors d'oeuvres, pouring beverages, and talking to Robbie and Henry about what they'd done that day. The boys picked out cupcakes they had decorated themselves.

Once the family was settled at a nearby table, Grace chose a cupcake for herself.

An odd noise, something between a sob and a cough, caused her to turn around. Danielle sat alone at one end of the veranda, a wineglass in one hand and a tissue in the other.

Grace perched on the edge of the chair next to her guest. "I'm sorry I didn't see you over here. Can I get you something? Perhaps some fruit or a cheese plate?"

Danielle sniffed and shook her head. "Food doesn't solve all the world's problems, you know." At least her light tone softened the rebuke behind her words.

"No, but it certainly helps. Think about all the tubs of ice cream that have been eaten after a bad breakup." As soon as the words were out of Grace's mouth, she wished she could take them back. She didn't know if Danielle was here to heal from a broken heart. If she was, Grace could join her in eating two tubs of moose tracks.

"I'm sorry. That sounded flippant." Grace paused, trying to find the best words to express what she wanted to say. Perhaps the simplest ones were the most profound. They were all she had. "You're obviously going through something. I don't want to pry or stick my nose where it doesn't belong. But if you need a friend, if I can help in any way, I want you to know I'm here."

Danielle lowered her eyes and pursed her lips. "You didn't like me very much when we worked together, did you?"

Grace picked at the paper surrounding her cupcake, but didn't remove it while she thought about how to answer Danielle. Surely, such a direct question deserved a direct answer. "No, but I'm not part of that world anymore. You're my guest, and I want you to feel at home here. To feel safe."

Tears glistened in Danielle's eyes. "Am I safe here?"

Grace didn't know what was behind Danielle's question, but her instinct for compassion and her gift of hospitality immediately surfaced. "Why wouldn't you be?"

Instead of answering, Danielle focused her attention on the private table at the end of the veranda.

Grace followed her gaze. Luke and Kaydi talked quietly at the table. A moment later, they got up and wandered arm in arm toward the rose garden.

"I've already met Kaydi," Danielle said. "Who's the guy she's with?"

"Luke Brannick. He lives in Magnolia Harbor."

"I didn't realize she was here to visit her boyfriend."

"They met a few days ago," Grace answered. "At an estate sale, I believe."

A sad smile crossed Danielle's face. "Does love at first sight really exist?"

"I don't know." Grace set the cupcake on the small round table situated between their chairs. "They do seem taken with each other."

"I hope they'll always be as happy as they are in this moment." Danielle took a sip of her wine. "I suppose we need the bumps and valleys to appreciate the mountaintops."

"Are you all right?" Grace asked.

"Don't worry about me. I'll be fine. My road is just a bit rough right now." Danielle stood. "A hot bath in that lovely tub is exactly what I need. I'll see you in the morning."

"If you get hungry later or if you want a sandwich or a snack, come down to the kitchen," Grace offered. "We always have something in the fridge."

"Ever the gracious hostess. I do appreciate that about you. Maybe now that we're not working together, we can be friends."

"I'd like that," Grace said.

"I would too." Without another word, Danielle left the veranda.

Grace sat back in the chair, reflecting on the strange conversation. If only Danielle would open up. Whatever was bothering her might be eased by talking about it. Or perhaps the burden was too personal.

Was it possible that Danielle was dying?

The thought slammed into Grace's mind, and she quickly pushed it away. Surely not.

Oh, Father, please don't let it be that.

Grace

Grace stood by the front desk and hit the buttons on the landline to listen to the message again. It had been years since she'd talked to the vice president of operations at Maddox Creative. No surprise there. They'd never been close. His voice was friendly—almost too friendly—as he greeted her.

"Hi, Grace. This is Franklin Hendrix. Long time, no see." Cordial laughter followed.

Grace thought his laughter sounded a little forced.

"I know this must be a surprise," Franklin continued. "Me calling out of the blue like this. I'm following up on a hunch and wanted to see if you could help. I'm sure you remember Danielle Holloway. After all, she accepted your position when you left. Not to get into the whole story on voice mail, but Danielle took an unexpected leave of absence, and I've got something going on here that I really need to discuss with her. Is there any chance she ended up at your B and B?"

He hesitated. "We had a few folks talking about what a nice place it was at the water cooler the other day"—again the forced laughter, maybe because there was no water cooler to gather around—"and, well, I don't know. Just thought I'd give you a call to see if she's there or if you've heard from her. Please call me back as soon as you can. This is very important." He recited his phone number, said goodbye, and disconnected.

For an instant, Grace wavered between saving and deleting the message. Better to have it and not need it than need it and not have it, she decided. She saved it and set down the receiver.

At least now she could be reassured that Danielle wasn't dying. Her troubles must have something to do with Maddox Creative.

If Franklin thought Grace was going to deliver Danielle up on a silver platter, he was sorely mistaken. Grace had a strict policy regarding guests at her inn. She never told outsiders whether someone was staying with her. It felt like a breach of confidence. If Danielle had taken a sudden leave of absence at work, she must have a good reason. At least this gave Grace an excuse to talk to Danielle about whatever was bothering her. Franklin had involved Grace, and even if Danielle wanted to keep her troubles to herself, Grace now had another opportunity to offer her assistance.

First, she had to find Danielle. She wasn't in her room. Grace had refreshed the suites before checking voice mail, and all of them had been unoccupied. The Zemas were kayaking, and Jack and Melissa were exploring the area. Kaydi had been noncommittal about her plans, but Grace assumed she was spending time with Luke.

Danielle hadn't mentioned her plans at breakfast when everyone else was sharing about their day. Maybe she was at the grandfather stump again. Or in the rose garden.

"Winston!" Grace called.

The little shih tzu came running.

She scooped him up and accepted his exuberant licking. "Would you like to go for a walk?"

When she set Winston back on the floor, he spun in a circle, barked, and spun again as if to say, "I'm ready. Let's go!"

Grace laughed, then set out for a little exploring of her own with Winston at her side. Hopefully she'd find Danielle without too much trouble. She searched the shoreline and waved to the Zemas. Robbie and

Henry loved the water, and their joyful shouts echoed from the lake.

Together, Grace and Winston wandered among the roses, then headed along the path to the sundial. "There's only one more place she might be, and that's the grandfather stump. Maybe the mystery man will be there again too."

Just in case, Grace scuffed her feet and stepped on a twig. If the mystery man was wary of her presence, she wanted to give him ample warning of her arrival. Though this might have been the opportunity to find out who Danielle was secretly seeing, Grace didn't want to operate that way. She needed to earn Danielle's trust. Danielle definitely wasn't going to readily give it. Perhaps she'd been burned too many times before.

As Danielle had been quick to point out, the two women hadn't exactly been friends when they worked together.

Grace hadn't thought about the final incident in ages—the one that had left such a sour taste in her mouth where Danielle was concerned—until Danielle had shown up at the inn. Grace had been certain that her protégé, Heather Fuller, was in line for the VP position. Especially after Danielle hadn't managed to sign that big account. It always seemed strange to Grace that Danielle had been rewarded with the corner office and all its perks despite her failure.

While poor Heather had her hopes dashed.

"You don't know how glad I am to be away from that drama," Grace said to Winston. "I wish it hadn't found me again."

She made her way past the three sisters, the trio of pines on the edge of the copse, and found Danielle sitting on the bench near the grandfather stump. She continued staring at the horizon and didn't acknowledge Grace's presence.

Winston jumped onto Danielle's lap. She cradled him and scratched behind his ears.

Grace sat beside her but didn't say anything. The quiet moment seemed to envelop both of them in its serenity. A gentle breeze stirred the branches of the nearby trees, and Grace involuntarily shivered.

"I think this is my favorite place at the inn," Danielle finally said. "It's so peaceful and happy somehow."

"Before lightning struck the tree, there was a tree house in its branches," Grace said. "The granddaughter of the people who owned the mansion before we bought it stayed with them during the summers. This was one of her favorite places too."

"Perhaps it's the echo of her laughter that I hear in the treetops." Danielle gazed upward as if she could envision the giant oak before it had fallen. "I suppose that makes me sound rather fanciful."

"I felt something like that the first time I saw this estate," Grace said. "Maybe the emotions experienced in a place linger there somehow. I believe there was a lot of love here. I hope there still is. Between Charlotte and me and with Aunt Winnie and Uncle Gus."

And Spencer. Grace closed her eyes.

"I'd like to believe that," Danielle said. "It brings me a kind of peace I hadn't expected to find."

"I'm sorry that I may have news that will disturb that peace."

Danielle took a deep breath, as if bracing herself for bad news. "What happened?"

"Franklin Hendrix called this morning."

Danielle's face went white, and her body stiffened. "You talked to him?"

"No, he left a message." Grace shifted sideways in her seat and rested her arm on the back of the bench. "I haven't called him back yet. I wanted to talk to you first."

Danielle's shoulders slightly relaxed, but her face muscles still appeared tense. "You can't tell him I'm here."

"He said he needs to talk to you."

"I can't. I won't." Danielle covered her face with her hands. "He wants to have me arrested."

Grace's heart dropped to her toes. "Arrested? For what?"

"Oh, I'm in the most horrible mess."

A million questions raced through Grace's mind, and she ignored them all. This was the time to listen, not talk. Her best move right now was to be quiet and allow Danielle the space and time she needed to tell her story.

"They think I stole winning tickets in a sweepstakes promotion," Danielle admitted.

"That's ridiculous. You'd never do such a thing." *Would she?* Grace shook her head. Danielle was too smart and ambitious to ever do something so foolish. Besides, stealing tickets like that was practically impossible. After that scandal with a top fast-food chain, practically every advertising agency in the country, Maddox Creative included, had put in even more safeguards to ensure any sweepstakes were won fair and square.

"I'm being set up," Danielle said.

"By who?" Grace asked.

"I don't know." For the first time, Danielle met Grace's gaze.

The sadness in her eyes was overwhelming, and Grace saw honesty there too. If Danielle was lying, she was an amazing actress.

"Someone at Maddox is involved," Danielle said. "Someone has to be."

"Could the theft have occurred with the accounting firm?"

"The client has its own accounting department, but someone there is involved too. We know it."

Grace raised her eyebrows. "We?"

"He's too afraid to ask anyone for help," Danielle said. "I've tried to tell him we can't figure this out on our own, but he's terrified. Even if we can clear our names, he could still go to jail."

Grace could hardly process what Danielle was telling her. It all sounded so strange. Sweepstakes were governed by so many laws, both federal and state. Why would anyone try to rig one? Beyond that, why would Danielle's mystery guy go to jail if he were innocent? "I don't understand," she finally said, and it felt like the understatement of the year.

"He was able to get certain documents as evidence," Danielle explained. "But he inadvertently downloaded other files. They'll accuse him of corporate espionage just to send a message to anyone else who might want to air their dirty laundry."

"Who's the client?"

"I can't tell you that. I've said too much already."

Grace wasn't surprised that Danielle refused to divulge the name. It was a question she shouldn't have asked. Still, it all seemed unbelievable. "This is a serious allegation. Your reputation and your position at the firm are in jeopardy."

"I know. I'm ruined unless we can figure something out. But until Ace—" Danielle stopped and bit her lip. "There's nothing I can do. Not yet."

"Who is Ace?" Grace asked gently.

Danielle didn't answer. Her profile seemed set in stone, almost as if she'd stopped breathing.

Grace considered asking her again, but what would be the use? No doubt he was the man who'd disappeared into the trees when Grace showed up here. The same man Winnie had seen with Danielle at The Book Cottage.

Grace's mind whirled. Even if Danielle was innocent, that didn't mean Ace was too. Apparently, he was the accountant who worked for the client. What if he had dragged Danielle into his own mess in the hopes of hiding his thievery behind her stellar reputation? And when that hadn't worked, convinced her to go on the run with him?

Grace couldn't ask Danielle those questions. Not if she wanted Danielle to trust her.

In Grace's experience, silence often worked wonders when someone was troubled but had doubts about voicing those troubles. If nothing else, the silence would provide Danielle with breathing space while Grace's presence assured her that she didn't need to face her problems by herself.

Grace momentarily closed her eyes and let her body relax against the hard slats of the bench. She inhaled the fragrance of the wildflowers growing by the grandfather stump and listened to the songs of birds as they flew from one limb to another. This was a lovely spot, one she didn't frequent as often as she should. Perhaps she could talk to Charlotte about building a gazebo around the stump. They could add colorful cushions to the benches. Grace let her mind drift away from Danielle's startling news to sink into her own tranquil moment.

All seemed at peace, and then Winston yipped and leaped from Danielle's lap.

Grace opened her eyes as he chased a squirrel up a tree. The squirrel seemed to scold Winston from its high perch while the small dog stood guard below.

"At least it's not a skunk." Danielle's voice held a trace of humor, but her expression remained stoic.

"I hope he never gets near a skunk again," Grace said. "I still smell that horrid odor sometimes, and I don't know if it's real or my imagination."

"Hopefully your imagination."

"I tossed out everything I was wearing that day." Grace shook her head as the memory of the reeking smell on her waterlogged shirt returned. She knew she could never wear it again without being reminded of that skunk's revenge on her dear little dog.

"I would have too." Suddenly Danielle clutched Grace's arm. "Please don't return Franklin's call. I'm begging you."

"I won't," Grace assured her. "There has to be something we can do. This isn't going to go away on its own."

"I know that." Danielle released Grace's arm and clasped her hands in her lap. Her knuckles turned white. "It's hard to know what steps to take. We have only one chance to prove our innocence, so we have to be careful."

"Doesn't running away make you look guilty?" Grace asked.

"I'm sure it does," Danielle said. "But I'm not guilty, and neither is Ace. Taking those other documents was an accident."

The documents could be—should be—returned. Why hadn't they been? Grace squirmed in the seat as she thought of a reason. "Are you planning to use them as some kind of bargaining chip?"

"Maybe." Danielle's tone sounded doubtful. "I don't know. That hadn't occurred to me."

"Maybe it occurred to Ace," Grace suggested.

"He's a good man. The best. He only wants to protect us." Danielle wrung her hands, then shifted to face Grace. "Please don't tell anyone where I am. Will you promise?"

"You're safe here." Even as she said the words, Grace wondered if they were true. She prayed so. At Danielle's stricken expression, she forced a reassuring smile. "As safe as anywhere else, I suppose."

"I knew I could count on you. When Ace said he was coming to Magnolia Harbor, I decided this was where I needed to come too. It almost seemed like God was guiding me." Danielle flexed her fingers and leaned back with a sigh. "I'm sorry we weren't friends before."

"Me too." Genuine warmth broadened Grace's smile, but her insides churned as the gravity of the situation and Danielle's request sunk in.

Danielle hadn't said anything about being arrested or having a warrant out for her arrest, so Grace didn't think she was harboring a fugitive. Even if she was, what could she do? Ask Danielle to leave? No, she could never do that. She'd just have to try to convince Danielle and Ace that the best option for both of them was to do what they could to clear their names.

But not at the moment. Danielle didn't seem to be in the mood to consider that approach. For now, Grace wouldn't push for action. Instead, she would do her best to ease Danielle's fears and earn her trust. "I'll keep your secret as long as possible, but you have to know that you can't hide here forever."

"I know." Danielle's voice was quiet. Barely a whisper. "Thank you."

"You're welcome."

There had to be a solution to this problem—there was always a solution. Grace was determined to find it.

14

Kaydi

Kaydi retrieved her phone from her pocket and opened her contacts. Julep Buckley's name appeared on the screen. All she had to do was push the button and make the call, but something seemed to stop her. After all, she had already left one message that hadn't been returned. Why should she leave another?

Since Luke needed to get started on the Townsends' sculpture, Kaydi had gone to the Jackson House Museum. Becky Thomas, the docent, hadn't been able to locate any Emmetts or Pipers in her records. She promised to keep searching, but Kaydi didn't hold out much hope.

Julep Buckley, Magnolia Harbor's walking historian, was about the only lead Kaydi had left. Unless she wanted to return to the boring newspaper archives and the microfiche machine.

Nope, she definitely didn't want to do that.

Kaydi frowned and took another sip of her caramel frappé. The creamy concoction was exactly what she needed, and the Dragonfly Coffee Shop was adorable. She'd been lucky to arrive when it wasn't too crowded, so she'd been able to snag a spot in one of the comfy chairs in the corner.

She set the phone on the table and stared out the window. She'd come to Magnolia Harbor for one purpose—to find out more about her grandmother. But as much as she was interested in solving that mystery, the search itself no longer appealed to her.

What did that say about her? About the kind of person she was?

It was something she'd been struggling with her entire life.

Kaydi didn't fit the mold of dutiful daughter. Of dutiful family member. She hadn't submitted the application to the Miss Omaha contest her mother insisted she enter until after the deadline. Her application was disqualified, not that Kaydi cared. Or how about when she'd refused to accept the scholarship from that East Coast liberal arts college because it was too far from home? Her grandma had understood but not Kaydi's parents.

Her mom had envisioned Kaydi winning pageants, and her dad had dreamed of a doctor in the family.

Beauty pageants and academia were not for her. And neither was combing through old newspapers and microfiche films. She didn't have the attention span to continue the tedious task for hours and hours, especially when it seemed unlikely that she'd find anything.

Maybe Kaydi was flighty. Just like her mom always said.

At least her grandmother had never minded when Kaydi flitted from one thing to another. She said Kaydi had the heart of a butterfly, fluttering in a delightful garden of colorful possibilities. The sign of a true creative. One week bookmaking and the next month mosaics. After that, ceramics. Her grandma encouraged all of Kaydi's interests, whether they lasted a day or two or a month or years. Like jewelry design. Kaydi might still dabble in other artistic pursuits, but she always returned to her passion—giving new sparkle to vintage jewelry.

That was why her grandmother had given Kaydi her butterfly necklace. As a reminder that the world needed butterflies.

Winnie strolled past the window of the coffee shop, and Kaydi spontaneously knocked on the glass.

The older woman startled, then smiled. She patted her chest as if to still her heart and went to the door of the shop.

Kaydi met Winnie at the counter. "I didn't mean to frighten you.

I was just so surprised to see you, and before I knew it, I was pounding on the window to get your attention."

"No harm done," Winnie said. "You gave me an excuse to indulge in a treat."

The energetic woman with long dark hair who'd waited on Kaydi earlier emerged from a back room and warmly greeted Winnie. "What kind of drink can I whip up for you today?"

"Whatever it is, it's my treat." Kaydi held up her hand to stop Winnie's attempt to protest. "It's the least I can do after scaring you half to death."

"I must have missed something," the barista said. Amusement danced in her light-brown eyes. "Is everything okay?"

"It is now," Winnie told her. "Have you and Kaydi been introduced?"

"Not officially. I'm Angel Diaz." She extended her hand. Henna tattoos scrolled from near her knuckles and along her arms, adding a rich luster to her already beautiful olive complexion. "Let me guess. You're staying at the Magnolia Harbor Inn."

"How did you know?" Kaydi asked.

"You're new to town, and you know Winnie." Angel grinned. "As simple as adding two and two."

Angel's bubbly personality encouraged Kaydi to feel even more welcome in this small-town community. How often had she gone to the same coffee shop in Omaha without ever experiencing such friendliness? The staff never remembered her name or treated her with such warmth.

"Are you enjoying your stay?" Angel asked.

"Very much." Memories of the past three days—almost every waking hour spent with Luke—whirled around her. After last night's hospitality hour, Luke had shown her the sculptures he'd created for the inn. Then they'd played board games with Jack and Melissa. They were also in their late twenties, just like Luke and Kaydi, and had been married for three years.

A little while later, Charlotte and Dean had invited the four of them into the kitchen to make individual gourmet pizzas from scratch. They'd all had so much fun rolling out their crusts and choosing their toppings. Kaydi learned how to grate cheese properly while Luke excelled at chopping onions and peppers.

Such a wonderful evening.

It was close to midnight when Kaydi had walked with Luke to the dock. Part of her hoped he would kiss her good night. Instead, he wrapped her in a tight embrace, then hurriedly hopped onto his boat. She'd seen the longing in his eyes and wondered if he'd seen the same in hers.

The coffee shop door opened as several people entered. Their boisterous conversations shook Kaydi from her reverie. Both Winnie and Angel stared at her, bemused smiles on their faces, and her cheeks warmed.

"She has the look," Angel stage-whispered to Winnie. "Anyone I know?"

"That's Kaydi's secret." Winnie set her lips in a straight line, but her hazel eyes sparkled. She glanced at the menu board and ordered a cup of jasmine tea.

"Coming right up," Angel said, then winked at Kaydi.

Not that Kaydi would have minded telling Angel about the days she'd spent with Luke. She'd gladly shout her feelings for him from the rooftops if only she could be sure he shared those feelings.

Angel handed Winnie her tea with a smile and turned her attention to the newcomers.

Kaydi returned to her corner seat.

Winnie settled into the neighboring chair and placed her shopping bag on the floor. "I picked up a few things at Spool & Thread before our Busy Bees meeting tonight."

"What's a Busy Bee?" Kaydi asked, amused by the name and thankful that Winnie had tactfully changed the subject.

"Our quilting group. We meet every Tuesday evening at six to quilt and gossip." Winnie gestured toward the counter. "Angel is our youngest member."

"I love her henna tattoos," Kaydi remarked. "I'd like to try that sometime."

"She'd probably paint on the henna for you. When she's not working here, she freelances as an illustrator." Winnie took a sip of tea. "I have a feeling you and Angel are cut from the same cloth, so to speak. Angel with her henna tattoos and you with your sparkling rings and jewelry. Both of you are free-spirited and creative."

Kaydi warmed to the compliment. "Thank you for saying that like it's a good thing."

"Why wouldn't it be a good thing?" Winnie asked, appearing puzzled.

"I don't know." Kaydi released a sigh. "I guess it's because the world has certain expectations. Traits like ambition and persistence are rewarded. Those of us who flit around like butterflies aren't always as valued."

"In other words, your drummer plays a rhythm for you that's different from most other people?" Winnie asked.

"You could say that." Kaydi wrinkled her nose and grinned. "Except it's such a cliché."

"It's an apt one. Besides, just because you march to a different drummer doesn't mean your song isn't as beautiful as anyone else's." Winnie smiled. "I have four daughters, and one of them—Maria—reminds me a lot of you. And of Angel, though Maria has no tattoos. At least none that I know about."

"Would she tell you if she did?" Kaydi asked.

"I'd like to think so," Winnie said. "Maria is both ambitious and persistent when it comes to her personal interests. When she's asked to do something she's not interested in, she's learned to say no rather than disappoint with a lackluster effort. We had the hardest time getting her to study science and geometry in high school, but she loved her literature and art classes."

"My parents would say the same thing about me." Kaydi nestled deeper into her comfortable seat. She enjoyed Winnie's company so much. Maybe because she reminded Kaydi of her beloved grandmother. How Kaydi missed her.

"I'm sure your parents are very proud of you," Winnie assured her. "It takes a special talent to see beauty that other people miss and to make that beauty a reality."

"I suppose they're proud." Kaydi knew they cared deeply about her despite their differences. Like Luke, she'd had a happy childhood, one she wouldn't trade for anything. She released a small sigh. "Sometimes I get the feeling that they think the jewelry design is a stage I'm going through, and they're being patient until I get a so-called real job."

"I'm sure they only want what's best for you," Winnie said. "Give them time to realize you're the best judge of what that best is."

Kaydi smiled. "You're a very wise woman."

"I try," Winnie said lightly, but she appeared pleased with the compliment.

Maybe Winnie was wise and understanding enough for Kaydi to confide in. When she'd imagined coming here, the secrecy of her quest added to the appeal of her trip. She'd envisioned herself as the mysterious person who came to town, asking questions, finding out things, without letting anyone know what she was doing—like a real-life detective. Now she had to admit the bloom was fading from that imaginative rose.

She took a deep breath and jumped in. "My grandmother came from here. Callie Jo Emmett Piper. Any chance you've heard of her? Or any of the Emmetts?"

"Can't say that I have." Winnie seemed to be searching her memory. "What else can you tell me about her?"

"Not much. At least not much about her life here. Neither of my grandparents ever talked about their childhoods. When we asked questions, they'd always brush them aside as if the answers weren't important. It almost seemed like they were hiding something, though we didn't really want to believe that. Until . . ."

"Until what?" Winnie prompted.

"My grandpa died about ten years ago. So we lost our chance to learn anything from him. Then about a year ago, my grandma started suffering from dementia. She'd forget who we were or where she was. She told us stories of these fabulous parties and luxurious dresses. At first, we thought she was making them up because my grandparents were never very well off. But the stories seemed so real to her. I came up with a theory, but she died before I could find out if I was right or not."

Winnie's eyes shone with compassion. "What's your theory?"

Kaydi took a deep breath. This was the moment to say out loud what she'd been surmising all these weeks while planning her trip. "I think Grandma was a true Southern debutante. The pampered and indulged daughter of a prosperous family. I believe her family disowned her when she eloped with the gardener's son."

"Oh my." Winnie sat back in the chair. "That's a story straight out of a romance novel. I'm sure it would have been quite the scandal in its time."

"You've never heard anything about it?"

"No, but that doesn't mean it didn't happen." Winnie cocked her head. "Have you talked to Julep yet?"

"I left her a message, but she hasn't called me back," Kaydi said.

"Can you tell me about any of the old estates in the area?"

"So many of them in this part of the country are gone now, though several have been given new life," Winnie answered. "A few are now bed-and-breakfasts like the Magnolia Harbor Inn, and others have become tourist attractions. There are only two or three I know of that still belong to an old family."

Kaydi could kick herself. Why hadn't she confided in Winnie that very first night? Then she might already have her answers. There was no use wishing for what couldn't be. At least she had a possible lead without spending more time with the microfiche machine. "Can you tell me about them?"

"Well, let's see. There's the Norwood estate, where you went to the sale."

"I don't think it's the right one."

"There's also the Orniston place," Winnie said. "It's a small museum now, but it doesn't get many tourists because it's off the beaten path. An Orniston ancestor was a physician, and one of the rooms is set up as it would have been when he used it as an examining room." She frowned. "Some folks seem interested in that sort of thing."

"I'm not sure if that's it," Kaydi said. "I like quirky museums as much as the next person, but old-fashioned doctor's instruments don't sound particularly appealing to me. On the other hand, my personal preferences don't mean that my grandma wasn't related to the Ornistons. I suppose I should visit it just in case."

"There's also Foxsong Meadows," Winnie continued, "but you'd know all about that."

"Foxsong Meadows? I've never heard of it." Or had she? There was something familiar about the name.

Winnie blinked in surprise. "I guess I misunderstood. I thought Grace said you and Luke Brannick were spending time together. And weren't you thinking of Luke a few minutes ago when you seemed to be in another world?"

"Guilty." Kaydi blushed. "I don't understand the connection."

"Foxsong Meadows is Luke's home," Winnie explained. "It's been in his family for generations."

Kaydi stared at Winnie, then directed her gaze out the window. *Foxsong.* In her memory, she heard her grandma whispering something about a folk song over and over again, her words not making any sense. Had she been saying *foxsong*?

It couldn't be possible. Luke couldn't be related to Grandma.

"Oh no," Kaydi croaked. "If my grandmother and Luke are related, then that means that Luke and I are too." Her throat seemed about to close, and she grabbed her frappé and sucked it down. The cold caramel drink somehow helped her regain control of her emotions.

"Haven't you already talked to Luke about why you're here?" Winnie asked.

How could Kaydi explain this was something she'd wanted to do on her own? It all seemed so silly now. Maybe she really was as flighty as her parents thought. "I only told the people who might help me find the answers. The librarian. Becky Thomas at the Jackson House Museum. The clerk at the newspaper." She couldn't believe she'd let her own imaginative fantasies keep her from confiding in the one person who might hold all the answers.

"So you didn't tell Luke?" Winnie asked gently.

"No, I wanted to figure out the mystery on my own," Kaydi answered, her voice filled with regret. "I can't keep looking though, not now."

"I doubt you and Luke would be near relations," Winnie said. It was obvious the older woman tried to sound comforting, but she furrowed her eyebrows. "There were usually daughters and very few sons at Foxsong Meadows, so it's hard to keep track of the family names.

But that doesn't mean your grandmother was one of them."

"What if she was?" Kaydi asked.

"You should talk to Luke. Or try to call Julep again."

"No," Kaydi said. "I don't want to know. I just want to go home."

"Go home?" Winnie patted Kaydi's arm. "You can't do that. What would you tell Luke?"

"That something came up. That my parents need me." Even as Kaydi said the words, she knew she couldn't do it. "I really like him. I more than like him."

"From what Grace tells me, I think he more than likes you too."

"What am I going to do?"

"You're going to talk to him," Winnie said firmly as if the decision had been made. "See what he knows about his family's genealogy."

"I'm scared of what I'll find out," Kaydi admitted.

"You'll find out the truth, and isn't that what you want? What you need?" Winnie gave her an encouraging smile. "It seems to me that you've been spending a lot of time with the one person who may have all the answers you're been searching for. Isn't that just like God, to give us what we need by putting it right in front of our faces?"

"Luke is taking me to dinner this evening." Kaydi's spirits had sunk so low that she didn't know if she could get out of the chair. Maybe she'd be stuck in the coffee shop forever. "I hope he's not related to my grandma."

"You'll know after you ask him. Then you can decide what's best to do." Winnie patted Kaydi's arm again. "Maybe it will turn out that your grandmother is related to the Ornistons. Or someone I'm not even thinking about."

"I hope you're right," Kaydi said. But deep down, she was positive that her grandmother was part of the Foxsong Meadows family. She'd finally found her grandma's connection to Magnolia Harbor.

A connection that might just break her heart.

15

Danielle

The map Danielle picked up at the visitors' center near the entrance to Prescott Park guided her along the winding narrow trail through the woods to the old factory ruins.

Ace sat on a partial wall next to a fallen chimney. "It's a good thing I have such a flexible job," he said as Danielle drew near. "You pick the most out-of-the-way places for us to meet."

"You're the one who insists we shouldn't be seen together." Danielle folded the map and perched beside him. "I'm doing my best to respect your wishes."

"I know this is hard, but please understand—"

"I talked to Grace," she interrupted. It was a relief to say it.

He gaped at her. "You did what?"

"Franklin Hendrix, the VP of operations, is searching for me. He left her a message."

"Grace told him where to find you." Ace's eyes widened with fear, then with hurt. "Are you leaving? Is this goodbye?"

"Grace hasn't returned his call. At least not yet." Danielle gazed around the ruins. This would be an interesting place to explore under different circumstances. According to information she'd read on the map, the factory had been built by Jeremiah Prescott after he discovered rich veins of clay. His highly regarded pottery had been exported to England back in the day.

"Do you think she will?" he asked.

Ace's question brought Danielle back to the present, and it made her stomach churn with apprehension. "She said she won't, but what if he comes here? It doesn't seem like anywhere is safe."

"I imagine Grace has policies in place to ensure the privacy of her guests," Ace said, clearly trying to sound reassuring, though Danielle noticed the small tremor in his voice. "Besides, you're more than a guest. You're a former colleague. A friend."

"We were never really friends," she said.

"She's being a friend to you now, isn't she?"

Danielle nodded. She briefly closed her eyes, praying he'd understand. "I told her about the theft of the sweepstakes."

The muscle in Ace's jaw twitched as he clamped his mouth closed. Somehow his silence was worse than if he had yelled at her.

"I didn't tell her about you," Danielle assured him. "At least I didn't tell her your real name. I'm sorry, but I couldn't help it. I've had all this bottled up inside me, and when she said that Franklin had called, everything came spilling out."

"What exactly did you tell her?" His voice was unnaturally steady.

"I told her we have proof of a theft and other information that we shouldn't have." Danielle tightened her grip on the map, then set it on her knee and pressed out the wrinkles.

"How did Grace respond?"

"She asked if the other files were a bargaining chip. I hadn't thought of that before, but maybe they could be. A way to get us out of this mess."

Ace pushed off the wall and stood in front of Danielle. "I've considered that, played out all kinds of scenarios in my mind. The bottom line is they need a scapegoat, and that's me."

"Maybe not," she suggested. "Perhaps if we called—"

"What would we say?" Ace asked, interrupting her. "'I'll give you the information I took if you'll just let me have my job back and not to arrest me. I promise I won't tell anyone about the stolen sweepstakes pieces.'" He placed his hands on his hips and lowered his head. "That's not going to happen. Not in a million years."

Danielle reached out and gripped his arm. "We can't go on like this. You know we can't. Charleston isn't that far from here, and we're not in a witness protection program or anything."

"You're right," he said. "I feel like we're trying to hide in plain sight."

"You don't want to do this forever, do you?" she asked, lightening her tone. "Wouldn't you rather go back to crunching numbers? Balancing spreadsheets? Creating fiscal reports?"

"It's not as boring as you're making it sound. There's a beauty, an order, in the numbers all balancing the way they should." Ace ran his hand along the rough bricks of the fallen chimney as if he could find his inner strength hidden in what remained of the structure. "But, no. I don't want to go back to that kind of high-stress environment. I'm still dreaming of that cabin in the wilds somewhere out west. Maybe I'd open a little bookkeeping business. Every Friday afternoon, I'd lock up and go fishing."

"I didn't know you liked to fish."

"I don't know that I'd like it either, but it would be a fun thing to try." He smiled at her, a sad but hopeful smile. "I haven't had fun in a long time."

"You're working too hard," she chided.

"My cousin said the same thing at breakfast," Ace said. "He doesn't know about all the times I sneak away to meet my accomplice-in-crime."

"Don't even joke about that," Danielle said firmly, though she couldn't help but smile.

For a few minutes, neither of them spoke.

Then Ace returned to his seat beside Danielle. "What about you?"

he asked. "Assuming we come out of this unscathed, will you open your own marketing firm? Or will you return to Maddox Creative?"

"I worked hard for that corner office. Harder than I'd ever worked before. I belonged there. But now? I wouldn't mind being my own boss." She took a deep breath. "Maybe go fishing on Friday afternoons."

Now Ace had to realize she had feelings for him. As much worry and sleepless nights as this situation had caused them, there had been a silver lining. They'd gotten to know each other in a way few people ever did.

He was so practical and self-assured that she scarcely dared to hope that he shared her growing feelings. She was practical enough to admit what she was feeling for him could be a reaction to the stress they were under. Right now, the two of them were alone against the whole world. Perhaps she was mistaking survival mode for romance.

Danielle was also honest, and she knew her feelings went much deeper than that. Once this nightmare was over—if it was ever over—she prayed their relationship wouldn't end.

Romance had never been on her radar, especially not after a bad breakup with her college sweetheart right after graduation. In her mind, the logical next step had been marriage and settling down together, but he'd had other plans that didn't include her.

Since then, Danielle had focused primarily on her career. She dated sometimes, but she never let anyone get too close. No one was going to get in the way of her pursuit of professional accomplishments.

Now that she had the corner office she'd dreamed of for so long, she still wasn't content. She loved the creative side of marketing, of bringing new products to consumers and discovering the message that resonated with an audience, but there was too much of a downside in the boring meetings, personal agendas, and company politics. She was weary of it.

And then this had happened. She'd gotten embroiled in a scandal and, like Ace, she feared that if Maddox Creative needed a scapegoat, they'd gladly select her.

"We don't have to wait till someday to go fishing," Ace said. "Why don't we go this Friday afternoon? I'm sure my cousin has all the gear we need."

"Fishing where?" she asked.

"On Lake Haven."

Danielle stared at him. "Do you think that's wise?"

"I think we both need to worry about something besides our careers," he said.

"And staying out of jail."

"Yeah, that too." Ace gently bumped her elbow. "What do you say? Shall we give fishing a go? See how good we'd be at it."

She tried to imagine herself out on a boat in the middle of the lake, casting a line into the water and reeling it back in. Maybe catching something. Maybe not. Perhaps Grace would help her prepare a snack for the excursion. Could Danielle and Ace really forget all their troubles for a couple of hours? There was only way to find out.

"Why not? I'll bring the food."

"I'll get the bait."

"Are you talking about worms and slugs?" she asked, cringing.

He laughed, a marvelous sound that swooped into her heart and lifted it up. "I'll even bait your line for you."

"No, I'll do it," Danielle said. "I won't like it, but I'll do it."

"You're a brave woman." They were simple words, but the expression in his eyes told her that he wasn't only talking about fishing.

"You're brave too."

Ace took her hand in his, his expression somber. "Then why am I hiding?"

"Because you're smart."

"I'm glad you think so. But you may be right. Perhaps it's time to stop."

It had been what she wanted—for the two of them to face this together. Yet now that he suggested it, Danielle felt a sense of trepidation. Whatever they did could backfire. Badly. "We have to be smart about that too," she reminded him.

"I know." Ace released a deep breath. "I don't want to go to jail."

"Let me talk to Grace."

"Not yet," he responded. "You may think I'm brave, but I need to find more courage first. Like the Cowardly Lion. Maybe I should visit the Wizard of Oz."

"If I remember the story correctly, the Cowardly Lion had the courage he needed all along. He just didn't know it."

"Not until Dorothy helped him to find it."

She squeezed his hand. "I'm not Dorothy, but I'm here for you."

Instead of saying anything, he bent his head toward hers.

She gazed into his eyes until the moment his lips touched hers. Then she closed her eyes as she lost herself in the bliss and thrill of their first kiss.

16

Luke

Luke removed the welder's helmet and took a step back to scrutinize his work. Patrick Haney, whose company handled the Norwood estate sale, had delivered the sugarcane crusher and post driver earlier that morning. Since then, Luke had scrubbed and polished the post driver, doing his best to clean the implement. He didn't want to mar the integrity of the piece, but it needed the added strength of the metal rods he was welding onto the rear to hold the crusher.

"I like it."

At the sound of the familiar voice, Luke whirled around. "Kaydi, what are you doing here?" He hurriedly shut off the welder, then slipped off his gauntlets. His mind whirled as he tried to settle on one feeling. Dismay that she'd shown up without an invitation? Happiness at seeing her again? Embarrassment because he hadn't told her about the family estate?

He glanced toward the large dilapidated mansion and the shadow it cast across the unkempt lawn. He mowed the grass once a week in the summer to keep it at a manageable height. But who had the time—or money—for weed control and aeration and fertilizer for such a large tract of land?

Not him.

"I'm sorry. I should have called first." Kaydi gave an apologetic smile and glanced around. "So this is Foxsong Meadows."

"That's right." He returned the smile. One feeling rose above the muddled others. Happiness. Her unexpected visit brightened an already bright day. "Some ancestor gave the place that name. There are still foxes around but probably not as many as when the house was built."

"How long ago was that?" Kaydi asked.

"Early 1800s." He waved his hand in a grand gesture toward the house. "As you can see, the family isn't as flush as we once were. Nor as prominent in local society."

She regarded the mansion. "Do you live here alone?"

Luke pointed at the gatehouse. "I live there." The squat rectangle, made of the same brick as the main house, had been updated after he decided to make it his home. The original windows had been replaced with larger ones that let in more light while retaining the historic charm. Luke was proud of the work he'd done on the building and proud to call it home. But what would Kaydi think of it? "It's much smaller and easier to maintain. Would you like to see inside?"

Kaydi seemed to hesitate, a darkness shadowing her eyes, but then her smile brightened.

Luke realized her smile seemed forced. What was wrong?

"Sure," she said. "I'd love to."

He led the way into the gatehouse and breathed a quick prayer of thanks that he'd washed the breakfast dishes that morning. As part of the renovation, he'd removed a couple of walls. Unlike before, the interior was bright and airy, and the spacious living area flowed seamlessly into the tidy kitchen with its creamy walls and stainless steel appliances. The leather furniture and mahogany wainscoting on the fireplace wall gave the place a masculine vibe.

"What do you think?" Luke asked.

"It's great." Kaydi's smile appeared more genuine now. "And it suits you. If I had to decorate a home for you, I would have come up with something similar."

"I'm glad you like it." He gestured toward a doorway. "The bedrooms and bathroom are down there. It's small, but it's home."

"Small?" Kaydi laughed. "I've lived in apartments smaller than this." She gestured around the living room and kitchen area. "I suppose when you've lived in a mansion, anything else would be considered small."

"Have a seat." Luke motioned to one of the two tall stools at the kitchen counter.

Kaydi sat down.

"We lived in the main house until Dad died." He leaned against an adjacent counter. "Then Mom decided she didn't want to stay there anymore because there were too many memories. So the two of us got a small place in town for a while. After I went off to college, she met my stepfather, and they moved to Florida. When I decided to move back, I fixed up this place instead of moving into the main house."

"Too many memories for you too?" she asked.

"No, not for me. My family had a lot of good times in that house." Luke shrugged. "My reasons are far more practical. I'm comfortable here in the gatehouse, and I can afford to keep up this part of the estate. The rest of it is too much. Too expensive. Too time-consuming. Too everything."

"I envy you," Kaydi said.

"Don't. I mean, I wouldn't trade the life I had in that house for anything, but now it's a burden. We don't know what to do with it."

"It would have been such an adventure to live in a place like that." Kaydi's eyes took on a dreamy expression that melted Luke's heart. "All those rooms. All that history."

"Unfortunately, when it's your life, you tend to take it for granted," he said. "I think it would be nice to see it through someone else's eyes." *Your eyes.*

"When was the last time you were inside the house?" she asked.

"I'm embarrassed to say how long it's been." Luke straightened and removed two glasses from a nearby cupboard. "Where are my manners? Would you like something to drink? I've got sweet tea. Brewed in the sunshine like it should be, with plenty of ice cubes."

"I'd like that," she said. "Thank you."

Luke busied himself preparing the tea, then led the way to the side porch. "Let's sit out here. There's usually a cool breeze because of the trees on this side and the paddle fans."

Once they were settled around the wicker table, he lifted his glass. "Here's to a breath of sunshine brightening my day." He grinned. "Did that sound too corny?"

Kaydi laughed. "It sounded wonderful."

Luke thought he'd never tire of hearing her laugh, hearing her voice.

"I know I should have called," Kaydi said. "I'm sure around here it's the height of rudeness to show up at someone's home unannounced."

"I don't mind," he said honestly.

Kaydi stared at him, her gaze direct as if she could see inside him. Then she stared down at the glass in her hand. "I was talking to Winnie earlier. She told me about Foxsong Meadows. At least what little she knew."

"I'm sorry I didn't tell you myself." How could Luke explain why he hadn't? He let out a long breath. "Sometimes when people find out that my family has been around the same place for so long and once owned a plantation, it changes how they think of me. It's easier to forget all that and pretend it's not part of who I am."

"I understand."

"I didn't mean to deceive you," he continued. "It just seemed like there were too many other things to talk about."

"We do tend to have a lot to say to each other." Her voice sounded wistful, and she wouldn't meet his eyes.

Luke frowned. Had he done something wrong? Said the wrong thing? "Are you mad I didn't tell you?"

She shook her head.

"Then what's the matter?"

Kaydi finally met his gaze. "I haven't been completely honest with you either."

"About what?" Realization slammed into his chest. "You have a boyfriend."

"What? No, of course not."

"Then what is it?" he asked.

"It's about why I'm in town." She closed her eyes and took a deep breath.

Luke didn't say anything. Grandpa always said a good man gave a woman all the time she needed. He might as well settle in to listen.

Finally, Kaydi opened her eyes.

Luke tried to decipher the emotions in their brown depths, but his heart didn't want to acknowledge their sadness.

"I don't even know where to begin," she admitted.

"The beginning?"

"I guess that's as good a place as any, but I'm not even sure where the beginning is."

"Make your best guess," he said quietly.

"Here goes." Kaydi set her glass on the table and shifted in her seat to face him. "I'd never heard of Magnolia Harbor until shortly before my grandmother died. My grandparents were always very secretive about their pasts. Though that isn't quite right. They didn't talk about the past, but I don't suppose we showed much interest. At least not until it was too late. They both were only children as far as we knew. Their parents had died. So we were their family. The only family they seemed to want or need."

She paused as if to gather her thoughts, then continued. "In the months before my grandmother died, her memories started getting mixed up. We'd start reminiscing about one thing, and she'd slip into a story about something none of the family knew about."

"What kind of story?" Luke asked.

"All kinds. She talked about elaborate parties and how she wore a long, elegant gown to the debutante ball. She'd mention these luxurious trips as casually as if she were talking about going to the grocery store. The thing is, my grandparents never traveled. I don't believe they'd been out of Nebraska since before I was born."

"That doesn't mean they didn't travel when they were younger," he reasoned. "Were her parents wealthy?"

"Not that we knew," Kaydi answered. "She did mention Magnolia Harbor. I looked it up in an atlas and showed her the map. She got very weepy and retreated into her own little world. I felt awful. She said something about being sorry, but she'd made the right choice no matter what anyone else thought. She'd lived a good life." She hesitated and stared at her feet. "A couple of minutes later, she didn't even know who I was."

Luke took her hand. Despite the warmth of the day, her fingers were chilly, and he rubbed them for warmth. "That's how it is with dementia. My grandfather is still as sharp as a tack, but there are others at the facility where he lives who have mental lapses. It's hard on their families."

"It is," Kaydi agreed. "I could never be sure what was real and what wasn't."

"I'm sorry your grandmother went through that."

"Me too." Kaydi started to smile at him, but then she froze. It was as if she remembered she had more to tell him. Something she didn't want to say.

A cold knot formed in Luke's stomach, preparing him for whatever was coming next.

Kaydi squeezed his hand. "A few times she murmured something that was hard to understand. I thought she was saying *folk song*, but after talking to Winnie, I think she was saying something else." She gazed at Luke expectantly, as if willing him to finish the thought for her.

For a moment, his mind spun. Then the connection snapped into place. "Foxsong?" He cocked his head. "You think she was saying *Foxsong*?"

"I'm sure of it."

Luke's heart plummeted into his stomach. Had Kaydi's grandmother lived at Foxsong Meadows? "What was her name?" He braced himself for the answer.

"Callie Jo Piper. Her maiden name was Emmett. Do you know it?"

Luke shook his head, relieved. "I'm not an expert on the family tree, but I don't know of any relatives by either of those names."

"Could there be?" Kaydi persisted.

The knot in his stomach tightened again. "When are we talking about? When would she have lived here?"

"I don't know. Maybe the 1940s or the 1950s."

"That's a long time ago. Our family names changed almost every generation." At least he knew that much from the stories his grandfather had told him.

"Winnie told me that." Kaydi loosened her grip on Luke's fingers, but she didn't let go. "More daughters than sons, she said."

"Probably one of the reasons for the instability of our finances," he muttered.

"What does that mean?" she asked, indignation coloring her tone. "That women can't handle money as well as men?"

"No, I didn't mean that." Luke laughed to cover his embarrassment for his unintended slight. "In those days, the husbands would have taken over the finances. It seems they were often more concerned about what the money could do for them than preserving it for the future."

Kaydi's eyes sparked. "Not my grandma. She and my grandpa only had what they earned." She took another deep breath. "I think he was the gardener here or maybe the son of the gardener, and they eloped."

He grinned at the idea. "A Foxsong heiress giving up her fortune for true love? That must have been a scandal," he said lightly.

"So you've never heard anything about it?" Kaydi asked, her tone remaining serious. "It seems like there would have been family stories."

"Like I said, I haven't been very interested in the family history." Luke swept his arm in the direction of the main house. "This place is like an albatross around my neck. I don't want to be the one to sell it, but what else am I supposed to do with it? Even if I did put it on the market, who would buy it? I don't want Grace and Charlotte to get another competitor in the bed-and-breakfast market, not that anyone could truly compete with them. Besides, the area doesn't need another museum or historical attraction. Most importantly, I don't want to move from this gatehouse."

"You have lots of reasons to keep it in the family." Kaydi bit her lip and turned away. Her hand slipped from his.

"Sentimental reasons," he said. "Maybe sentiment runs in the family. Another reason we lost our fortune."

They sat in silence for a few moments.

The knot in his stomach tightened even more. Again, Luke had the uneasy feeling he'd said the wrong thing. Or that he'd missed something he should have seen. Then like a lightning bolt, it hit him. He lifted her chin till their eyes met. "Are you afraid we're related?"

"We might be."

"Even if we are, we'd be what? Second cousins? Something like that."

"If we have the same great-grandparents, yes, we'd be second cousins."

"Does that make a difference? To us?"

"Shouldn't it?"

"No." Luke grasped for something to say, something to reassure her, even though she was right. Being related made all the difference. "Maybe that's why we had such an instant connection."

"Maybe." Kaydi got up. "I'm going back to the inn now. It's been a long day. A hard day."

Luke stood next to her. He couldn't let her go. Not yet. "Why don't you stay? I'll clean up, and we can go exploring. We have a date for dinner, don't we? We can go to Aunt Patsy's Porch. The head waitress, Molly, wants to meet you and tell you what a great guy I am." He knew he was rambling, but he couldn't seem to stop it.

"That all sounds really great," Kaydi replied wistfully. "But I don't think that's a good idea. Spending time with you . . . I can't. Not anymore."

Luke bit his lip and hung his head. He didn't want her to leave, but he didn't know how to convince her to stay.

Second cousins. They couldn't be.

Could they?

It was definitely time for him to find out more about his family tree.

Grace

The sun shimmered, hot and bright, on the waves of Lake Haven. Another ideal afternoon to be out on the water. Grace handed two children's life vests to Mandy. "The boys sure are loving the kayaks this summer."

"They definitely enjoy the lake," Mandy said. Even braided, the young mother's thick dark hair reached almost to her waist. She gazed toward the bank where Chet and their boys were playing with Winston. When she turned back to Grace, a sad smile flitted across her delicate features. "I can't believe it's Wednesday already. This week is going too fast. It seems like we just arrived, and in a couple of days, we'll be leaving again."

"Are you sure you can't stay through the weekend?" Grace asked. That had been the family's original plan, but a personal matter had come up so they had to shorten their stay. Grace was sincerely sorry to see them go. She and Charlotte had come to regard the Zemas as family over the years.

On their first visit, shortly after the inn opened, Mandy and Chet had left Robbie at home with his grandparents for a romantic getaway. During the stay, Mandy had learned her upset stomach was actually morning sickness. Charlotte pampered her with special broths and teas while Grace treated her to a day at the spa.

The next year, they came back with Robbie and baby Henry. The tradition continued, and Grace and Charlotte looked forward to their arrival each summer so they could see how much the boys had grown and catch up on their family news.

"I wish we could spend an entire month here." Mandy walked with Grace to the bank.

Seeing their mom headed their way, the boys raced to the docks where several kayaks were lined up and ready to take out into the lake.

"This is one of my favorite places," Mandy said. "Except for home, of course."

"Of course." Grace and the younger woman had that in common. In a way, they were both homebodies, even though Grace had an inn to run, and Mandy operated a small bakery from her home that specialized in gorgeous cakes and other scrumptious desserts.

The women chatted while Chet got the boys into their vests. Before long, he was in a red kayak with Henry while Mandy and Robbie took the blue one. The boys shouted goodbye to Grace and Winston as they pushed away from the shore.

She waved to them, and Winston stood on the bank and barked.

Grace scooped him up before he decided to go for a swim. "Do you wish you could go with them?"

Winston yipped his reply, and Grace snuggled him close.

Truth be told, she wouldn't mind going out in the kayak herself, but then she'd have to shower and change before hospitality hour. There wasn't enough time, especially if Charlotte needed her help preparing the appetizers. However, it wouldn't hurt to sit and enjoy the sunshine for a few moments. She settled into one of the Adirondack chairs near the dock. Winston stretched out beside her.

Besides, her real motive for taking out the kayak would be to recapture a memory that shouldn't be recaptured. Memories were like that. They were lived once and relived in imagination but never repeated. Something would always be different. Like that old saying running through her head now. *You can't step in the same stream twice.*

Though it would be nice to return to the day that beckoned her.

The Saturday before Valentine's Day, she and Spencer had taken the kayaks out onto the lake despite the cold and blustery weather. "An unseasonable adventure," he'd called it. Then on Valentine's Day—no. She wouldn't relive that memory either.

Nor the memory of Hank's astonishing appearance back from the dead.

She pressed her forehead against her arms. When he returned, her tranquil life had transformed into a soap opera. Except this wasn't a television show but real life. Her real life.

And her heart was in turmoil because of it.

Not because she still loved Hank but because she wanted to love Spencer.

"Mind if I join you?"

Spencer. Every muscle in Grace's body tensed, and her senses heightened. She glanced up at him, shading her eyes against the sun. Dark lenses hid his eyes, but the gentle curve of his lips and the tightness of his jaw revealed his uncertainty.

Bailey, Spencer's chocolate Lab, greeted Winston.

"Please." She gestured at the chair next to her. "Have a seat."

Spencer sat down beside her. Bailey pushed her head against his hand, and Spencer rubbed the dog's ear. "Great day for being on the lake. Did you go kayaking without me?"

"Not me. The Zemas." She pointed to the red and blue kayaks.

"I ran into them at the ice cream shop the other day and got a chance to catch up on their news," he said. "The boys have really grown."

"They're still as adorably rowdy as ever."

"As boys should be." Spencer tapped the arms of the chair with his fingers.

That was an uncharacteristic gesture for him. Was he nervous?

"Are you all booked up?" he asked.

"Yes." Grace cringed at the shortness of her answer. Why couldn't they have a conversation anymore without feeling awkward? Stilted? They'd been friends too long to be uneasy around each other.

"Anyone interesting?"

"All our guests are interesting in their own way." She inwardly groaned. She'd done it again. Why couldn't she be herself instead of sounding so horribly pretentious? That wasn't her. That wasn't them.

Except there wasn't a *them*. Not anymore.

"I've been gone for a while," Spencer said. "Seems like I'm out of touch with what's going on around here."

"Oh?" So that was why she hadn't seen him around. Even if he'd been home, would he have stayed away from the inn? From her?

"The girls and I took an impromptu road trip up the coast. It's been a long time since we've done anything like that. Just the three of us." He cleared his throat. Apparently, he felt as uncomfortable as Grace did.

"That sounds like a great adventure," Grace said, pushing enthusiasm into her tone. "It's nice they could both get away at the same time."

Spencer's daughters shared an apartment in Charleston. Kylie, the elder by two years, worked as a physical therapist, and Megan was a flight attendant. They were a close family, but the young women's schedules sometimes made it difficult for them to get together with their dad.

"It took some finagling, but it was worth it. A good trip." He let out a breath, then repeated softly, "A good trip."

The wistful tone in his voice tugged at Grace's heart. But she couldn't give in to those kinds of feelings. Not now.

"You haven't missed much around here," she said too brightly. "I can't think of even the tiniest bit of local gossip to tell you."

"Grace!" Charlotte called.

Grace glanced behind her.

Charlotte jogged toward her, waving a slip of paper. When she reached them, she fanned herself with the paper to catch her breath. "Hey, Spencer. I didn't know you were here." Her gaze darted to Grace. "Hope I haven't interrupted anything."

"Nothing at all," Grace said. "What's going on?"

"Phone message for you." Charlotte handed the paper to Grace. "Franklin Hendrix from Maddox Creative. He said it was important that he talk to you as soon as possible."

Grace's stomach clenched. "You didn't leave him on hold, did you?"

"Of course not. I told him I'd give you the message right away." She appeared doubtful. "Isn't he a vice president or something? He's not offering you another position there, is he?"

"Vice president of operations," Grace replied. "No, it's nothing like that. Not that I would go back even if he did."

"That's good." Charlotte's expression instantly changed from alarm to her usual joy. "I'll leave you two alone. I've got brownies in the oven. Will you be joining us this evening, Spencer?"

"I don't think so. Thanks for the offer, though. I appreciate it."

"You know you're welcome anytime," Charlotte said, then glanced at her sister. *Isn't he?* The unspoken question was as clearly written in Charlotte's eyes as if she'd asked it out loud.

"Thanks for the message," Grace said. "I'll be there soon to help get things ready."

"No rush. I have everything under control." Charlotte trotted back toward the mansion. "I mean it," she called over her shoulder. "Take your time."

Grace and Spencer exchanged glances. For the first time since he arrived, he seemed more relaxed, and they chuckled together.

"Sisters," Grace remarked. "Can't live with them, and can't live without them."

"Not that you would want to," he pointed out, still chuckling.

"No, I wouldn't." Grace stared at the paper, then folded it and slid it into her pocket. The last thing she wanted to do was call Franklin. Why did he keep bothering her?

"You meant that, didn't you?" Spencer said. "You wouldn't go back to Maddox Creative no matter what they offered?"

"He's not calling about a job. It's something else entirely."

"You seem troubled," he said, studying her. "Do you want to talk about it?"

"No." She sighed. "Yes. Unfortunately, it's not my story to tell."

Spencer sat forward and shifted so he was sitting on the edge of the chair facing her. "If you change your mind, I'm here for you. You know that, don't you?"

She gazed at him, and he removed his sunglasses. Suddenly everything seemed to be the way it was before. Maybe not as it had been in the weeks before Hank showed up. But as it was months before when she and Spencer were very good friends. When they had fun together and their relationship was uncomplicated.

Almost before she knew what she was doing, she found herself confiding in him. "I have a friend. Not really a friend but a former colleague. Franklin wants to know where she is."

"You're avoiding his call because you don't want to tell him." It wasn't a question. Though Spencer had retired from the FBI several years ago, his deductive abilities remained sharp.

"That's right."

"Is your former colleague a guest at the inn?" he asked.

Grace hesitated, then nodded. "She's in trouble, and she doesn't see a way out. I don't know how to help her. Plus, there's someone else involved. A man."

"Is he staying here too?"

"He's been around, but he's not staying here. I don't know who he is. I saw him talking to Danielle once in the garden, but he left before I got close enough to see who it was."

"Could he be dangerous?" Spencer asked, sounding concerned.

"No, it's not like that," Grace quickly reassured him. "I don't want to say too much. It has to do with a corporate scandal."

Spencer released a sigh as if letting go of his worry. "Corporate crime. Even though it's usually not as violent or random as drug issues and smuggling, it can still get messy. Often there's big money at stake. I'd hate to see you get caught up in anything that could cause you trouble."

"I don't think Danielle means to put anyone in danger," Grace said. "She's only here because it's a place for her to hide."

"It seems strange that she'd come here." He raised his eyebrows. "Didn't you say you weren't close?"

"We were more like rivals when we worked together." Grace absentmindedly rubbed Bailey's head. The Lab had settled between their chairs. "She wasn't the person I recommended to take my place. In fact, I was surprised when Danielle was promoted to my position."

"You don't think she deserved it?"

"She's creative and a hard worker, but I'd been grooming someone else to fill my shoes. A kind of protégé, I guess you could say. I thought Heather was the clear pick for the position, but she and Danielle had an issue with each other. She told me that Danielle sabotaged one of her campaigns. There was no proof, so I didn't feel like I could bring it to my boss's attention without it looking like sour grapes."

"Have you talked to Danielle about it?" Spencer asked.

"Never. Back then it wouldn't have made any difference. If I bring it up now, it'll sound like I'm holding a grudge. Which I'm not."

"No," he said. "You're not the kind of person to do that."

Something in Spencer's tone, in the way he turned his gaze away from her, made Grace wonder if he was thinking about Hank. Did he think she'd been too easy on her ex-husband? Maybe. She didn't want to talk about Hank. Not with Spencer. Not with anyone.

"I don't have to tell you that there are two sides to every story. Sometimes more than that," Spencer said. "I hate to think she's putting you in a bad position here. Especially if she has done unethical things in the past. How do you know she's not lying to you now?"

"I don't, but she seems so frightened," she said. "If I'm the only person she can trust, then I need to be here for her."

"You have a good instinct about people," he said. "I've seen it again and again since I moved here. I think you can trust that instinct."

"Thank you," Grace said, smiling slightly. He couldn't have given her a nicer compliment. "I hope you're right."

Resting his elbows on his knees, he linked his fingers together. "Do you think she'd talk to me?"

"I don't know about that."

"It's not like I'm still in the bureau," Spencer reminded her. "If she told me the details about what's going on, I might be able to advise her. It sounds like she should talk to an attorney."

"I think she's afraid to talk to anyone," she said.

"Just let her know—if you think it'll help—that I'm willing to listen."

"That's very kind of you."

"Just being neighborly."

More than neighborly. A good friend. At least Grace knew she could always count on that. Whatever the future held for them, she'd forever be grateful that Spencer lived just down the road at Blossom Hill Farm.

And he would never do anything as disgraceful and dishonest as Hank had done.

Kaydi

As Kaydi entered the driveway to the Orniston family museum, she spied Luke leaning against the rear bumper of his truck. She parked her rental car next to him in the gravel lot in front of the stone cottage. She couldn't guess what the cottage had been used for during the estate's heyday, but now it seemed to be the visitors' center for the small museum. The stone mansion stood about two hundred yards away on a slight rise.

"I wasn't sure you were coming," he said as she stepped out of her car.

"I'm not late." She'd been watching the time on her dashboard. "Unless the clock in my car is wrong."

"No." He shrugged. "Guess I was just nervous."

"Nervous? Why?" Though Kaydi didn't really need to ask. She was nervous too. They'd talked for a few minutes on the phone this morning when Luke had called to ask her to meet him here at the other estate Winnie had mentioned.

Their conversation had felt stilted. Neither of them had been at ease. Her grandmother's possible connection to Foxsong Meadows had changed the free-spirited nature of their relationship.

"I'm anxious about what we might find out, I suppose," Luke admitted. "I'm also hoping this is where your grandma lived. Hoping you and I aren't related."

"I hope that too."

He gestured toward the cottage. "Shall we?"

"What if the guide doesn't know anything?" Kaydi asked. She momentarily closed her eyes. "I don't know what I'm going to say."

Luke took her hand.

She should have pulled away, but she didn't.

"I called Nelson Orniston this morning after we talked," he said. "He's meeting us here. Just tell him what you told me yesterday."

"I can do that." Hopefully a family member would have the information she needed to know.

They entered the cottage and were greeted by a perky teenager who was rearranging a display of souvenirs in the tiny gift shop area. "Welcome to the Orniston Museum." Her bright smile revealed two adorable dimples. "Hi, Luke. Mr. Orniston told me you were coming."

"Hi, Toni. I'd like you to meet a friend of mine. This is Kaydi Engstrom." Luke squeezed Kaydi's hand. "Kaydi, this is Toni Carter. She's our mayor's daughter. The oldest of five." He wiggled five fingers in the air and widened his eyes, making a silly face.

Kaydi elbowed him to stop his teasing. "It's nice to meet you. I'm an only child, so I have no idea what it's like to have brothers and sisters. Sometimes I wish I did."

"Sometimes I wish I didn't." Toni laughed, then pulled a key from her pocket and handed it to Luke. "The golf cart is around to the side. You can drive it up to the mansion. Mr. Orniston said he'd meet you in the library."

"Thanks," Luke said. "I appreciate it."

After promising Toni they would stop in before they left, Kaydi and Luke exited the cottage and found the golf cart. A broad winding path led from the visitors' center to the side of the mansion.

The squat three-story house wasn't as sprawling as Foxsong Meadows. Though it didn't have the brightness of the Magnolia

Harbor Inn, it was apparent that an attempt had been made to update the facade while maintaining its nineteenth-century charm.

When they entered the library, Nelson Orniston greeted them warmly, and Luke introduced Kaydi.

"Please have a seat," Nelson said, gesturing to the grouping of armchairs.

As Kaydi and Luke sat down, Nelson went to the sideboard and poured three cups of tea.

Kaydi gazed around the masculine room. Floor-to-ceiling bookcases lined three of the walls. Statuary and other objets d'art were interspersed among the leather-bound volumes. A sliding ladder was hooked on a rail at the top of one of the shelves. The fourth wall held magnificent portraits in large gaudy frames. A set of French doors led to a wide veranda.

"This has always been my favorite room in the house," Nelson commented as he handed Kaydi a cup of tea. "What do you think of it?"

"All these books are wonderful," she said. "Though to tell you the truth, I'm not much of a reader."

"Nor am I," Nelson admitted. "In fact, I'm quite sure many of them haven't been removed since they were first shelved. Except to be dusted, of course."

"That's sad," Kaydi said.

Nelson gave Luke his tea, then sat down in a nearby chair with his own cup. "I agree. Unfortunately, a library like this was more important in my grandfather's day than it is now. Even if the books weren't read, their mere presence spoke of social standing and education."

"And wealth," Luke added.

"True. It took money to gather so many volumes in one place," Nelson said. "But these old books aren't nearly as valuable now as they used to be."

"I find that hard to believe," Kaydi said. "You have hundreds of them."

Nelson shook his head. "No first editions. Nothing rare or sought after. Just the same gentleman's library found in most musty old mansions in the South."

"At least you've been able to hold on to your books," Luke said. "So have we, but the Norwoods dismantled their library long ago. Others have too."

Nelson murmured agreement as he dropped a sugar cube into his cup. "My grandfather was frugal. Some would say stingy. The legacy he left behind allowed us to make the transformation from home to museum. Now it's in the hands of the foundation to keep it running. It was the best way I had to preserve it."

"Do you still live here?" Kaydi asked.

"No, my wife and I have a place not far from the southeastern shore of Lake Haven," Nelson replied. "It's much more suitable for us, and it's a big draw for the grandkids. They love water sports, and we love having them visit. They'll be coming at the end of the month and staying until after the Fourth of July."

"This is definitely a great place to spend a vacation," Kaydi said.

"Luke tells me that you think you might have roots in the area," Nelson said gently. His expression told her he was ready to hear her story.

"Perhaps." She told him what she knew about her grandparents and about her grandma's odd stories. "Her maiden name was Emmett, and my grandfather's name was Piper. Do those names mean anything to you?"

"I'm sorry, but they don't. There certainly aren't any Emmetts or Pipers in our family tree. Genealogy is one of my hobbies. I can show you the records." Nelson ushered them to a long mahogany table situated near one corner of the room. "Here are a few of our family charts."

For the next several minutes, he flipped through pages of a thick, cord-bound book with heavy brown pages. The charts showed different branches of the family. None had the names Kaydi had hoped to find.

That meant her grandmother could be related to the family at Foxsong Meadows. Which meant Kaydi could be related to Luke. Maybe Luke was right, and that was why they'd felt such a sudden connection. It wasn't love at first sight but a shared heritage that somehow drew them together.

It sounded impossible, but stranger things happened every day. If twins who had been separated at birth could feel a strong bond for each other after spending decades apart, was it so hard to believe that cousins would be able to feel a bit of the same thing? She'd mistaken a family connection for a heart connection.

So had Luke.

Kaydi gave him a sad smile, and he responded with an encouraging smile of his own that didn't quite reach his eyes.

Perhaps she should think about going home. It would be easier on her heart if she got on the next flight to Omaha. But she didn't want to leave Luke. Not yet. Even though being with him broke her heart, being away from him would hurt even more. Perhaps they could figure out the relationship that worked best for them.

Maybe family. Definitely friends.

Never a couple.

19

Danielle

At Grace's invitation, Danielle took the seat opposite her in the charming cottage where Charlotte lived. Danielle had tossed and turned most of the night. Shortly before dawn, she'd finally fallen into a deep sleep. By the time she awoke, she'd missed breakfast. Not that she minded. She didn't have much of an appetite these days.

Danielle had wandered into the music room, assuming it would be a private place to think. Who was she kidding? A private place to brood.

Grace found her there and suggested they take a walk. Winston trotted along beside them. The next thing Danielle knew they were entering the cottage.

Winston went over to a patch of sunshine and stretched out on the floor.

"This is a lovely home," Danielle said as she settled against the multicolored cushions on the upholstered couch. "Small but comfortable."

"Charlotte loves living here." Grace arranged molasses cookies on a plate and poured lemonade into two tall glasses. "As soon as we saw the property, she claimed it for her own. At first, I thought she was out of her mind because it needed extensive renovations, but now it's perfect for her."

"Is she going to join us?" Danielle asked.

"No, she's at the inn preparing delicious appetizers for tonight's hospitality hour." Grace set the plate of cookies on the coffee table and handed Danielle a glass and a napkin. "Will you be there?"

"Probably." Danielle took a sip of lemonade. "I have to admit that being in your sister's home without her seems rather odd. Do you invite all your guests to these kinds of private gatherings?"

"No, but she gave her permission." Grace sat in a nearby chair. "We need to talk, and we won't be interrupted here."

"I can't tell you anything more than I already have." Danielle released a heavy sigh. She wished she could give Grace additional details, but she refused to betray any more of Ace's confidence in her. She didn't agree with him, but she cared too much about him to do anything about their predicament without his cooperation.

"Actually, I wanted to talk to you about something else." Grace glanced down at her glass but not quickly enough. Her cheeks had reddened.

Was she embarrassed?

"Really?" Danielle tried to keep her voice calm, but she suspected the only thing Grace had to talk to her about was the calls from Maddox Creative. "You didn't return Franklin's call, did you?" Her voice rose to a shrill pitch. She hated the sound, but she couldn't seem to control it.

"What?" Grace asked, sounding surprised. "No, of course not."

Danielle remained silent as relief coursed through her.

"He called again yesterday," Grace said. "Charlotte took the message. I don't know how long I can avoid him, but I'm doing my best."

"What if he comes here?"

Grace stiffened. "We'll hide you," she said as if stating the obvious.

"You'd lie to him?" Danielle asked. "For me?"

"It's our policy." Grace seemed to swallow a sudden urge to laugh. "I don't mean it's our policy to hide people or to lie, but we don't give out information about our guests. Though I'm not sure I wouldn't give you away. That's why I haven't called him back." She shrugged. "I'm not a good liar."

"I understand." Danielle smiled slightly. "Neither am I."

Grace dropped eye contact and focused on her drink.

"I'm not," Danielle insisted. "Do you think I am?"

"Not a liar," Grace said. Her voice wavered. "Actually, that's what I wanted to talk to you about."

"You think I lied about something?" Danielle couldn't even imagine what it could be.

"Perhaps *lied* is too strong a word." Grace closed her eyes for a moment.

What her hostess had to say was obviously hard for her, but Danielle didn't want to make it any easier. Not when she didn't have a clue what Grace intended to talk about.

"Heather Fuller told me what happened with the See Me Now Sunglasses campaign," Grace said. "How you disparaged her presentation in front of the client when they preferred her ideas to yours."

Danielle sat back in her chair. Her mind seemed to go blank for a second as she tried to concentrate on what Grace was insinuating. Heather Fuller. Before arriving at the inn, Danielle hadn't thought about her in ages. Seeing Grace had brought back the circumstances regarding Danielle's promotion, but she had too many other concerns to give them much thought. Now she found it hard to believe what Heather had told Grace about her.

"I'm not sure you know the entire story." Danielle kept her voice down. She wanted to rant and rave, but that never did any good. It certainly wouldn't win her points with Grace, and she needed Grace to believe what she had to tell her. "You and Heather were close."

"I admit that I hoped—even expected—she would take my place as VP."

"Are you upset that they chose me instead?" Danielle asked.

"Let's just say I was surprised," Grace responded.

"Did you tell anyone else what Heather said?" Danielle held up her hand to stop Grace from answering. "No, you must not have. Or else I probably wouldn't be occupying that corner office."

"It would have been her word against yours," Grace said. "Obviously, they wanted you more than they did her."

"So you had made a mistake in judgment by championing Heather." Danielle hated the defensiveness in her voice. But the mention of the See Me Now Sunglasses campaign had broken her carefully constructed dam around the emotions she'd felt during that transition. The celebration of her promotion had been marred by Heather's accusations.

"Or they did." Grace's voice was quiet but firm.

Danielle laughed. An unattractive, unkind laugh that she immediately regretted. She was so stunned by the turn of the conversation that she hardly knew what to think.

Grace took a sip of her lemonade and remained silent.

"I'm not the liar," Danielle finally said, her voice steady with conviction. "Heather is."

"That's hard for me to believe."

"I know you liked her. You trusted her. She was your protégé." Danielle shook her head. "However, she's not as much like you as you thought she was. I'm sorry you didn't know."

"Know what?" Grace asked.

"Her missteps. Her mishandling of the See Me Now campaign and others before that one. I really tried to help her. I had no idea she would go to you and throw me under the bus."

"Are you saying you didn't undercut her?" The doubt in Grace's expression now seemed tinged with uncertainty.

"Heather created a compelling presentation," Danielle said. "It would have been great for a run-of-the-mill sunglass company, but See Me Now was about more than a single product. She didn't seem to understand their culture, their story." She pressed her hands together and took a deep breath. "I decided to exclude Heather's presentation from the client meeting. So she went behind my back and contacted the client to reschedule the meeting."

"Surely she didn't." Apparently, Grace had no idea. She was obviously shocked to find out what Heather had done.

"I happened to be in the lobby when the client's team arrived," Danielle continued. "I did my best to hide my surprise. Heather made her presentation, but the team wasn't impressed. I tried to salvage the meeting by bringing in a few idea boards, but it was too little too late. We lost the account."

"I am so sorry," Grace said. "If I had known—"

"It wasn't your fault," Danielle said, interrupting her. "Heather didn't want to listen to me, and she was so convinced she was right that she took matters into her own hands. That takes a certain kind of courage."

"She didn't have the courage to own up to her mistakes," Grace pointed out.

"No, she didn't," Danielle said, her voice soft. "But that's all in the past. I hope you and I can leave it there."

"We can if you'll forgive me for not coming to you when all this happened," Grace said. "It's what I should have done."

"Forgiven and forgotten."

A warm smile brightened Grace's expression. "I'd like for us to be friends."

"Me too," Danielle responded. Even though her other troubles still weighed her down, she was grateful that she and Grace had talked about Heather.

A certain kind of courage, Danielle mused as she bit into a cookie. Maybe that was what she needed to face her uncertain future.

Maybe it was what Ace needed too.

20

Grace

Winston had been stretched out in a patch of sunshine coming through one of the cottage windows. As if sensing Grace needed him, he left his spot and sat at her feet. She picked him up, finding comfort in his furry presence while she listened to Danielle's explanation of what had happened with the See Me Now Sunglasses account.

At first, Grace didn't want to believe what Danielle was telling her. As she listened, she realized that Danielle had to be telling the truth. For the first time, she acknowledged a few minor flaws in the story Heather had told her. Details she'd ignored at the time because they hadn't seemed important. On top of that, she had been exhausted from juggling the transition of her accounts before her last day at Maddox and making plans with Charlotte for the bed-and-breakfast they planned to open together.

Exhaustion and distraction weren't good enough reasons for being blind to what was happening with her protégé. Grace should have paid more attention to her instincts instead of letting her regard for Heather cloud her judgment. She released a heavy smile. "A friend recently told me that I have good instincts when it comes to people. I guess he was wrong."

"He wasn't wrong. We all have our blind spots." Danielle gave her a self-deprecating smile. "I may have one of my own right now."

"Your mystery man?" Grace asked.

Danielle nodded.

"The friend I just mentioned," Grace said. "He's retired FBI. He offered to help."

Danielle widened her eyes. "You told him my secret."

"I didn't give him any details." Grace placed Winston on the floor and joined Danielle on the couch. "I only said you needed help. I promise I betrayed no confidences. I wouldn't do that."

"I trusted you," Danielle said, her voice ringing with accusation and despair.

"I know you're scared." Grace placed a comforting hand on Danielle's arm. "I know Ace is scared. Now that Franklin is calling me, I'm scared too. Spencer is a good guy, one of the best. If you don't want to confide in me or a lawyer, he might be your best option. Please think about it. Give us a chance to do what we can to help you."

Danielle buried her face in her hands. After a few moments, she leaned back and clasped her fingers behind her head. "We do need help, but I'm not sure if I can convince Ace."

"Then maybe it's time for you to do what needs to be done," Grace said. "Ask Ace to meet with you, and I'll ask Spencer to join you."

"I don't know. Ace wouldn't like that."

"You realize it's the right thing to do."

Danielle held Grace's gaze. "Will you be there?"

"If you want me to be."

"I can't do this anymore, but if we aren't careful . . ." Danielle let the rest of the sentence hang between them.

"We won't let anything happen to you," Grace said, putting as much reassurance in her tone as possible. Was she making a promise she couldn't keep? She hoped not. But she had every confidence that Spencer would know how to advise Danielle and Ace.

Besides, Grace had even more reason to want to help Danielle. She'd let her affection for Heather affect her feelings for Danielle. That hadn't been fair, and she wanted to make it up to her.

"Thank you." Danielle's voice was quiet yet resolved. "I'll give Ace a call."

"I'm here for you."

"I know."

Winston whimpered and put his paw on Danielle's knee.

She picked him up with a smile. "Looks like Winston is on my side too."

"He knows a friend when he sees one," Grace said. "I'm glad you're here and that you're giving me another chance."

"It goes both ways." Danielle extended her hand as a mischievous smile lifted the corners of her mouth. "Accomplices?"

Grace grinned as she shook her hand. "Accomplices."

Luke

Something wasn't right. The sculpture that Luke had been working on most of the day was off-kilter somehow, out of balance. No matter what he did to fix it, it only seemed to get worse. He couldn't remember the last time he'd had so much trouble applying the vision in his head to the mass of metal and wood in front of him.

Anyone who knew about art had heard of Michelangelo saying that he simply took a piece of marble and chipped away everything that didn't belong to release the sculpture within.

Luke didn't claim to have the genius of the famed sculptor, but he understood the concept. He could see the treasure in what others called junk. He could see the possibilities in what others viewed as ordinary objects.

The vision for this piece had been clear when he'd bought the crusher and post driver at the estate sale. He'd been doing fine at making his vision appear for everyone else to see.

Until he and Kaydi visited the Orniston family museum yesterday.

Now it almost seemed like Luke was someone else. He was experiencing emotions he'd never experienced before. All because a cute brunette with dazzling eyes and freckled cheeks had disrupted his life by swooping in, stealing his heart, and running away.

The past few days had been a whirlwind Luke didn't understand, and he hadn't wanted to at first. Instead, he'd marveled at the idea that maybe there was something to love at first sight. Because as impossible as it sounded, it certainly felt like that was what had happened between him and Kaydi.

He would have scoffed at the thought a week ago.

Now he wanted—needed—to find out the truth about any kinship they might have to each other.

Luke sighed. There was no use trying to work anymore. He was getting nowhere, and if he wasn't careful, he'd do too much damage to the piece to fix it.

He put away his tools, covered the unfinished sculpture with a large drop cloth, and strode to the gatehouse, where he poured tea over a glassful of ice. He frowned at the glass, then squeezed lemon juice into the beverage. Lots of lemon juice.

Then he carried the glass to the porch and settled onto the cushioned glider. As he lifted his cell phone, it lit up, and the screen of icons appeared. He still wasn't sure what he was going to say to his mother. How could he explain the situation? Maybe the words would come to him.

After tapping the screen a few times, Luke hit the speaker button. Not wanting his mom to read more than he wanted in his facial expressions, he deliberately avoided a video call.

His mother picked up immediately. "What a nice surprise." Her cheery voice had an immediate calming effect.

"How are you doing?" he asked.

"What's wrong?"

Okay, maybe the calming effect wasn't as immediate as he'd thought. "Who said anything was wrong?"

"For one thing, it's the middle of the afternoon in the middle of the week, which is not your customary time for calling. And then there's your tone that says plain as day that you need your mama."

"I don't have a tone for that."

"Remember who you're talking to," his mother chided. "I've never been wrong about that tone."

"I promise you that nothing is wrong." Luke pushed the glider into motion with his foot. "It's just that things aren't exactly right either."

"What things?" she asked.

He took a deep breath and plunged ahead. "I'm going to tell you something, but I don't want you to get all crazy on me. Promise?"

"You met someone." A muted squeal came through the line.

Luke grinned and shook his head. Talk about mother's intuition. "Yes, I met someone."

"Tell me about her," she said. "What's her name? How did you meet? Can I talk to her?"

"Hold on a minute," he said. "One thing at a time, okay?"

"I already know she's special. She'd have to be to catch your attention."

"Kaydi is special." He released a heavy sigh. "She might also be related to us."

Silence. He could almost hear his mom's thoughts whirling around in her head.

"That seems unlikely," she finally said. "Our family tree has never been a broad one."

"I know." He told her about Kaydi's search for her grandmother's roots and her suspicions that they shared the same great-grandparents.

"I still don't see how that's possible," his mother insisted. "I've never heard of any Emmetts or Pipers."

"How could I find out?" Luke asked. "There has to be some kind of family record. A genealogy or something."

"Unfortunately, I was never too interested in all of that," his mom admitted. "I was surrounded by history every day of my life living in that mansion. The past seemed like a musty place compared to the future." She sighed wistfully. "Now I wish I had paid more attention to my parents' stories."

"Me too." He pushed the glider into motion again, harder this time. "I don't know what to do. Kaydi will be leaving soon, and I don't want to let her go."

His mother paused. "There was a big black leather Bible. I remember it had these colorful illustrations, like something out of medieval times."

"Do you have any idea where it is?"

"I'd start with the attic. Even if you don't find it, you'll probably run across some old photo albums. Kaydi might recognize her grandparents. Maybe you'll even find birth certificates or something like that. It couldn't hurt to take a peek."

The attic. Why hadn't he thought of that before? For the first time since Kaydi had expressed her fears of their possible family connection, Luke felt a glimmer of hope. "I'll give Kaydi a call and see if she wants to help me search."

"I suppose we should go through all the boxes and trunks and everything else stored in that house," she said. "It seems like such an overwhelming job. I hardly know where to begin."

"What are we going to do with the house?" he asked.

"I wish I knew. Selling it would seem like such a slap in the face to those who built it and lived in it. On the other hand, I know it's a burden for you."

"Do you think you'll ever come back?" Luke wasn't sure why he asked the question when he already knew the answer. Maybe because hearing it would allow him to let go of the place. At least a little bit more than he'd been able to until now.

"We're happy here," his mother replied, her voice low.

Luke could almost read her thoughts. She was happy, more than happy in her new marriage, but she never wanted him to think that she'd replaced his father or resent her new husband for not being Dad.

"I'm glad," he said. "I really am."

He sensed her smile as clearly as if he could see it. Now he regretted his decision to make this an audio call instead of a video call.

"When do you think you might make it down to visit?" Mom's voice had almost a false cheeriness to it. Mingled with just enough hope to keep him from feeling guilty if he blew her off. Or rather, to keep herself from being too disappointed.

"Before the summer ends." The answer surprised him. It wasn't what he'd meant to say.

It obviously surprised his mother too. "Do you mean it?" She sounded flabbergasted.

"I do." Another surprise. He did.

"Maybe you could bring Kaydi with you." She laughed. "Or is that hoping for too much?"

"I'd love for the two of you to meet," Luke said. "I guess it depends on what we discover in the attic."

"I'll be praying that you find no interconnecting branches. Not even the smallest twig."

"Thanks. You're the best."

"So are you."

He disconnected the call, then stared at the phone. Instead of calling Kaydi, he could go to the inn and see her in person. Perhaps talk her into going to dinner with him.

Luke shook his head. That wouldn't be fair to either of them. They would be awkward with each other as long as this huge unknown hung like a gloomy cloud over their heads.

He texted Kaydi. *Talked to my mom. She suggested I search through the attic for the family Bible. Want to help?*

Her reply came quickly. *Would love to. Tomorrow morning?*
I'll fix breakfast.
See you then.

Luke sighed. He looked forward to seeing Kaydi again, but he feared for what they might uncover during their search.

Kaydi

Where would they even begin? Would it really make a difference? Kaydi held in her frustration, not wanting Luke to see how overwhelmed she felt. Today was Friday. On Sunday, she'd be flying back to Omaha. Could they find anything worthwhile before then?

The attic in the mansion wasn't merely one large area separated by regularly spaced studs. It was a series of dark rooms crowded with furniture, floor lamps, dressmaker mannequins, boxes, tools, and other assorted objects. At least Luke had thought to bring light bulbs to replace the ones that had burned out. One of his ancestors had had the foresight to place the sockets at regular intervals along the ceiling beams. The corners held their shadows, but they had enough light to go through the drawers, trunks, and boxes.

"Do you think we'll find the Bible?" Kaydi asked.

"We will." Luke's voice held more bravado than confidence. "We have to."

"I don't think anyone in your family ever threw anything away. Have you considered restoring some of these pieces?" She removed the dustcover from a cherry washstand. "This is lovely."

"I've never thought about it," he answered. "When I talked to Mom yesterday, she said she wished she'd cared more about our family's history. I guess we're both regretting that we've neglected our heritage."

Kaydi examined the washstand. "It does seem like a shame to hide all these beautiful antiques away."

"You're right. For now, though, we need to focus on finding that Bible."

She glanced around. "Where should I start?"

"Go through the drawers of that washstand and everything else in that section," he said. "I'm going to check out this trunk. I remember it used to be in Grandpa's bedroom."

Kaydi opened the small door on one side of the washstand. "Wow, this even has the original chamber pot. It's in great condition except for a layer of dust."

The top drawer contained assorted combs, brushes, and perfume bottles. The two drawers next to the small door held washcloths and towels.

She wandered over to the trunk to see what Luke had found. He was flipping through a photo album.

"Grandpa's military photos. He was in Vietnam the last couple of years. Look at this." Luke pointed to a certificate affixed to one of the pages. "I never knew he got the Medal of Honor."

Kaydi waved her arm around the attic. "It's like there's an entire history here that no one knows about."

"It's too bad." Luke closed the album. "I never wanted to open this place up to strangers, but there's something kind of sad about the family memories being relegated to the top floor of the house. I understand now why some of these estates have become museums."

"You didn't before?"

He shrugged. "To be honest, I always thought it was kind of a low-class thing to do. Like they were saying, 'Look at me. I'm important.' Now I'm not so sure. It seems like a nice way to honor those who went before."

"Are you saying you want to turn this place into a museum?" After visiting the Orniston family museum yesterday, Kaydi couldn't imagine the time and effort that would take. Nelson had mentioned a board of trustees and a foundation for raising money. She had a hard time envisioning Luke wading through all the bureaucracy and red tape.

"Not really, but maybe there are things here that should be donated to the historical society." He set the photo album on a nearby table. "Not that, of course. I'm taking it with me so I can go through it later. But there are probably other things."

"Would your mom mind if you did that?" If not, that seemed like a good solution.

Luke shook his head. "She's never coming back. Not to live here anyway. I've been holding on to this place just in case Mom needed a home or I decided to raise my family here. But it's too much responsibility. Too much upkeep. Too much stuff."

"You don't have to make any decisions today." Kaydi gazed around the space. "I understand what you mean. There's way too much stuff here."

"Somewhere in this stuff is a Bible and maybe other photos," he said. "We need to find them."

The task seemed impossible, but if they were going to discover the truth about whether her grandmother had been a member of this household, they needed to keep searching.

Even as Kaydi hoped that her grandmother wasn't related to the Foxsong residents, she couldn't help imagining what life might have been like in those days so long ago. Though it wouldn't have been a happy life for everyone.

She didn't know if Luke's family had once owned slaves. She wasn't sure she wanted to know, but it seemed likely. That thought hurt a deep place in her heart. Not that Luke or his parents could be blamed.

The trouble with digging up the past was that Kaydi didn't know what she was going to find. One thing was certain. There was just as likely to be bad as well as good, tragedy as well as joy.

Kaydi and Luke were searching for the answer to one specific question. But what other questions would arise from their search? And what if the answers weren't what they wanted?

For the next hour, they rummaged through boxes and drawers. Luke had placed the contents of one sturdy box into an old wardrobe containing musty furs. Now he was using the box for items he wanted to take with him to the gatehouse.

After a break for lunch, they returned to another section of the attic.

Behind a garment rack of coats, Kaydi found a secretary desk with a drop-down lid in the hutch and three drawers in the base. She lowered the lid to reveal a few cubbyholes stuffed with papers and envelopes. "Do you think any of these could be important?" she called out.

Luke left the box he was sifting through to join her. "How important could they be if no one's bothered with them in all this time?" He closed the lid and opened the top drawer of the base, then whistled. "This might be important."

"What is it?" Kaydi asked.

He pulled out a large wooden box and smiled at her. "I think this is it."

The top of the box was engraved with a Scripture verse.

Thy word is a lamp unto my feet

And a light unto my path.

Psalm 119:105

Beneath the verse were the words: *Foxsong Meadows Estate.*

"The Bible?" Kaydi asked as a shiver raced up her spine.

"Let's see." Luke opened the lid. A thick Bible nestled inside the box. "We found it."

She gripped Luke's arm. "I'm nervous."

"Me too." He closed the lid. "Let's take this over by the window so we can see it better."

"I've got an idea." Kaydi scurried through the boxes and furniture until she found an old floor lamp. She grabbed one of the light bulbs that Luke had brought with him and carried both to the secretary desk. "Where can we plug this in?"

"Right over here." Luke led the way to an outlet. He exchanged the old bulb for the new one and plugged in the lamp.

Kaydi flipped on the switch. "It's not much light, but it'll help."

Luke made a makeshift stand out of a couple of boxes, then gingerly lifted the Bible from its protective box. The leather cover was worn and cracked from age.

"We should have taken better care of this," he remarked, sounding apologetic. "I don't even know how it got up here."

"At least we found it," Kaydi reminded him. "Hopefully we'll find out what we need to know."

"Here goes nothing." Luke carefully thumbed through the first few pages. "This is the list of family births. The first entry is from 1795. Wow. I didn't remember it went that far back."

"Are you mentioned?"

Luke turned the page and pointed to the last entry. "Here I am. This is my mom's handwriting." He rested his fingers lightly on the page. "It feels like it connects me to my family, to all of my ancestors who came before me."

"You're lucky to have something like this. I wish I did." Kaydi regretted those last words as soon as she'd said them. They were true but somehow selfish.

"Maybe it'll turn out this belongs to both of us." He frowned as he glanced at her. "I hope not."

"I hope not too."

"This is my mom and my grandmother," Luke said, pointing to their names. He ran his finger farther up the page. "These two names don't make sense. Look at the birth dates."

Kaydi peered at the writing. The name entered above Luke's grandmother's was Caroline Anne.

"Her date of birth was only about ten years before my grandmother's," he said, indicating the date. "So she can't be my great-grandmother."

"Maybe she's your great-aunt," she suggested.

Luke pointed to the name and birth date above Caroline's. "Jedidiah William. He's old enough to be my grandmother's father but too young to be Caroline's."

"My grandma was only a few months younger than Caroline," Kaydi said, her voice rising with excitement. "If she was part of your family, her name would have been below hers. We're not related."

Luke traced his finger along Kaydi's jaw, then lifted her chin. "We're not related." He pulled her into an embrace.

Kaydi rested her head against his chest. "I'm so glad," she whispered.

"Me too." He relaxed his embrace and clasped her hands in his. "You still don't know anything about your family, though. You're back to square one."

"Maybe I totally misunderstood," she said. "Perhaps my grandma meant a different Magnolia Harbor."

"Is there another one?" Luke asked.

"Not that I could find when I did an online search."

"Then we're not going to give up the search here," he insisted. "You still haven't talked to Julep Buckley, have you?"

"No, she hasn't returned my call."

"Then we'll call her again." Luke closed the Bible and returned it to the engraved box. "If your grandma ever lived in Magnolia Harbor, there has to be some trace of her. We'll find that clue together."

"You'll help me?"

"Try to stop me."

Kaydi was touched not only by his words but the tone of his voice and the warmth in his eyes. She felt her cheeks flush and butterflies flutter deep within her. It was hard to believe the way Luke made her feel inside, as if he understood all there was to know about her. That was impossible since they'd known each other for only a few days. But in that short amount of time she supposed they had shared more with each other than some people did during their entire lifetimes. It was as if they were always meant to know each other, to complete each other's missing part.

Yet the feelings were all so new, so tender. How well could they possibly know each other?

Kaydi knew Luke well enough to realize that she didn't want to leave him. She hoped he truly did feel as strongly for her as she felt for him.

They needed more time together. More time to know if this was real.

"Let's go through the rest of the drawers in this secretary desk while we're here and then call it a day," Luke said.

"What else are you searching for?"

"Nothing in particular." He picked up a photo album from the drawer and placed it in the box for items to take to the gatehouse. "But I want to take all of these."

Kaydi helped him pack the remaining albums and the Bible into the box.

"How about I pick you up in an hour?" Luke asked as he removed the bottom drawer of the desk and set it on a table. "We can grab a bite to eat."

"What did you have in mind?"

"Do you like pizza?"

"I love it."

He grinned. "I've got just the place. It's in Magnolia Harbor, and it's called Cappy's. They have the best pizza you'll ever taste this side of the Atlantic."

"That's a pretty bold claim," Kaydi teased.

"I stick by it. Will you be ready in an hour?"

"Better give me ninety minutes." She needed time to return to the inn and wash the attic dust out of her hair. A long hot bath would be nice too.

"Seventy-five."

"Seventy-five." Kaydi laughed. "You're not so bad at dickering after all."

While Luke sorted through the items in the drawer, she removed a handful of papers from a cubbyhole in the hutch. Even if Luke didn't think they were important, it wouldn't hurt to take a peek. As she did, a photograph slipped from the pile.

Kaydi picked up the photo and examined it. A woman with light-brown hair was dressed in a beautiful russet and gold gown with a scoop neckline and cap sleeves. Long white gloves covered her arms. She wore the same butterfly necklace that her grandma had given Kaydi, but this woman wasn't her grandmother.

She gasped, then peered at it closely, wanting to be sure. There was no denying it. The piece was too unique for it to be anything other than the original. She turned over the photo. Written in faded pencil on the back were the words: *Caroline at the harvest ball.*

How could Caroline have her grandma's necklace? Kaydi's heart threatened to pound through her chest, but she couldn't stop an unsettling thought from pushing through.

"I've got to go." She thrust the photo and the papers into the box and hurried toward the stairs.

"Wait a minute," Luke called after her. "I'll walk you out."

"No." She hurried on, doing her best to hold back her tears until she reached her rental car. It was impossible. Her grandmother could never have done such a thing.

But what if she had?

All the secrecy, all the distancing from the past. It made sense now. Whoever her grandma had been, she must have known Caroline.

Before she eloped with Kaydi's grandfather, she must have stolen Caroline's necklace.

Find Carrie Ann. Tell her I'm sorry.

Her grandmother's forlorn pleas whispered in Kaydi's ears as she steered onto the main road, her tires spinning gravel from the driveway. Not Carrie Ann but Carrie Anne. Anne with an *e*, just like Anne Shirley. It must have been her grandma's nickname for the Caroline Anne listed in the Bible. The Caroline dressed in a fine gown for an autumn ball.

Kaydi had found her grandmother's connection to Magnolia Harbor. What was her connection to Foxsong Meadows? Was it as dishonorable as it seemed?

Was everything Kaydi thought about her grandmother completely wrong?

23

Danielle

What a difference a day made. Danielle still couldn't believe how much fun she'd had yesterday afternoon visiting with Grace in Charlotte's cozy cottage. After they got past what had happened at Maddox Creative, the two women had chatted like old friends as they discovered they had similar tastes in books, music—especially old show tunes—and even vices. Ice cream was at the top of that list.

Grace had encouraged Danielle to attend last evening's hospitality hour and not to sit in a corner by herself. She'd had a lovely evening visiting with Chet and Mandy as their boys and Winston played ball in the grassy expanse near the veranda. Jack and Melissa had joined them too. For at least a little while, Danielle's mind was distracted by delicious appetizers and wine, amiable conversation, and the antics of the children and the dog. Her troubles weren't forgotten, but they no longer consumed her thoughts.

When Mandy mentioned at breakfast this morning that they'd be leaving later that afternoon, Danielle decided to get something to occupy the boys on their long drive home to Augusta, Georgia. She stopped in at The Book Cottage and purchased activity books, packs of colored pencils, and tote bags to store everything. She also spotted a book that Grace had said was on her to-read list, so she bought it as a token of her gratitude for all that her new friend was doing for her.

Danielle browsed through a couple of other stores, then noticed a truck with a familiar logo parked near the Dragonfly Coffee Shop.

Her heart raced, and she rested her hand on her chest to calm her jitters. Just because she'd seen Ace in the truck before didn't mean he was driving it today.

There was only one way to find out. She straightened her shoulders, entered the coffee shop, and searched the interior. There he was, sitting at a secluded table and reading a newspaper. Danielle approached him. "Fancy meeting you here."

At the sound of her voice, Ace lifted his gaze from the newspaper. A small smile brightened his face, but his eyes held their usual wariness. "What are you doing here?"

"I saw the truck outside." She rested her shopping bag on the table. "Mind if I join you?"

He rose and pulled out the adjacent chair. "I just ordered. Can I get you anything?"

Danielle sat down and glanced around the coffee shop. At this time of day, it wasn't busy. "Are you sure you don't mind us being seen together?"

Ace placed his hand on hers. "I'm tired of sneaking around and meeting in places like cemeteries and factory ruins. We're not criminal masterminds or members of the mob."

"If we were criminal masterminds, we'd be on a private island with millions in an offshore account," Danielle joked.

The barista—a man who appeared to be in his late thirties with brown hair that was short on the sides and long and tousled on the top—set a frothy concoction and a chocolate croissant in front of Ace. "Enjoy." He smiled at Danielle. "What can I get for you?"

"Danielle, this is Josh Ford, the owner of the Dragonfly," Ace said. "Josh, this is Danielle. She's a friend who's staying at the Magnolia Harbor Inn."

They exchanged pleasantries, and Danielle placed her order.

After Josh returned to the counter, Ace leaned toward Danielle. "Maybe it's time for me to call Conrad."

She was taken aback. "Your boss? You tried talking to him before." The chief financial officer's threats were what had prompted Ace to find refuge with his cousin in the first place.

"Maybe he's cooled off by now."

Danielle took a deep breath. "I talked to Grace yesterday. She has a friend who is retired from the FBI. Spencer Lewis. She thinks we should talk to him. He might have connections that can help us."

"What if everything crashes down around us?" he asked.

"We go on the lam," she teased. "Find that little cabin out west."

Ace tilted his head and smiled. "Would you really go on the run with me?"

"Probably not." Danielle returned his smile. "I'll stand beside you, though. No matter what happens."

"What about when this is all over?" Ace asked, holding her gaze.

She felt the rush of something new and wonderful surging through her. "I'll stand beside you then too for as long as you want me to."

He opened his mouth to speak, but nothing came out. His eyes conveyed what he couldn't put into words.

She put a hand on his arm. "I know."

Ace slowly nodded. "I'll meet with Spencer, but I'm not making any promises about what I'll do after that."

"I'm not asking you to." Danielle pulled her phone from her bag and searched for Grace's number. "We'll take things one step at a time."

And pray they lead to the end of this nightmare.

24

Kaydi

Her grandmother a thief? Kaydi didn't want to believe it—couldn't believe it—but what other explanation could there be?

Perhaps Caroline had given the butterfly necklace to her grandma. Then why would she have told Kaydi that story about visiting with the jeweler and designing the piece herself?

That meant her grandmother wasn't only a thief. She was also a liar. What else had she lied to Kaydi about?

Kaydi took a long shower to wash off the dirt and grime from the attic, but the hot water couldn't wash away the awful feelings whirling around inside her.

After the shower, she put on a simple sundress and gazed out the window. Her vantage point on the third floor provided a magnificent view of the lake.

A couple of boats bounced on the sparkling waves. She almost wished she was out there with them—as long as she had butter rum Life Savers with her. That day with Luke had been such a happy day. Every moment with Luke had been a happy moment.

Until now.

How could she ever explain to him that her grandmother had stolen something so valuable from his family?

There would be no more dates with him now. The best thing Kaydi could do was pack up and go home. She no longer wanted to know her grandmother's history. The elopement with the gardener's son, which had sounded so romantic, was now spoiled.

Was that why her grandma had taken the necklace? To finance her elopement? No, that couldn't have been the reason, or she wouldn't still have the necklace. What if she'd stolen other pieces of jewelry with it and sold those but kept this one?

The uncertainty and the horrible questions looped around Kaydi's brain until her head hurt.

As she stared out at the lake, a boat pulled up to the dock. A boat she recognized. Someone hopped onto the deck and secured the boat.

Luke.

She didn't want to see him, didn't want to have to tell him of her family's tawdry history. Yet there was nothing else for her to do. She would tell him about the theft, and then she'd pack her bags and go home. That was the best thing for both of them.

Luke walked toward the inn from the boat. As he neared the entrance, he glanced toward the third floor.

Kaydi felt like her heart was about to break. She turned away from the window. As much as she hated to put a blemish on her grandmother's name, Luke deserved to know the truth. Hopefully he wouldn't hold it against her.

And there was one more thing she had to do.

She took the butterfly necklace from her jewelry box. "Time for you to go back where you belong," she murmured. She slipped it inside a small box from one of the trinkets she'd picked up on this trip, which had been so wonderful at first.

Kaydi stopped in front of the mirror. If she was going to apologize and ask for Luke's forgiveness, she was definitely going to look as good as possible when she did so. She deemed her appearance appropriate for the occasion, then slid on her sandals, cradled the box containing the necklace, and left her suite.

Luke met her at the foot of the stairs and grinned. "You look lovely."

"Thank you." Kaydi frowned. "I'm sorry for leaving the way I did."

"It's all right," he said. "I think I know the reason."

"How could you?" she asked.

Luke glanced around the foyer. "Is there somewhere we can talk without being disturbed?"

"How about the living room?" Kaydi suggested.

"Perfect."

She led the way, and they sat down on the couch with a view of the lake.

"I want to show you something," Luke said.

"I have something to show you too," Kaydi said. "I'm so ashamed. I hardly know what to think. What to say."

His excitement faded into concern. "What is it?"

"I think this belongs to you." She held out the small box. "To Caroline."

Luke accepted the box and opened it. "This is the necklace you wore when we went to The Tidewater."

"My grandmother left it to me," Kaydi said. "I saw a photo of Caroline when we were in the attic. She was wearing this exact same necklace."

"I don't think she was."

"I know that piece like the back of my hand. Believe me, it's the same." She hung her head. "I'm so embarrassed. I would never have believed my grandmother could do such a thing."

"Your grandmother didn't do anything wrong," he told her.

"How can you know that?"

"Because of what I discovered after you left." Luke handed her a box. "Go ahead. Open it."

Kaydi reluctantly placed the box on her lap and removed the lid. Inside was a photo album. An inscription on the cover read:

Carrie Anne and Callie Jo

Best Friends Forever

"They were best friends?" she asked. "That makes it even worse."

"After you left in such a hurry, I saw the photo of Caroline you put in the box," Luke said. "I recognized the necklace too. I remembered seeing a box with Caroline's name on it in the trunk. That's where I found this album." He took it from Kaydi and flipped through a few pages. "Check out this photo."

The picture showed two young women dressed in long gowns. One was her grandma, and the other one was Caroline. Their bright smiles exuded youth and vitality.

Most importantly, they both wore identical necklaces.

"They both had one." Kaydi almost couldn't believe what she was seeing. That meant her grandmother hadn't stolen Caroline's necklace.

"They must have been very close friends indeed," Luke remarked.

"Yet Grandma never mentioned her. At least not until her memories were fading."

"Maybe they drifted apart."

"Or had a falling-out." Kaydi bit her lip and sighed. "My grandma asked me to find Carrie Anne and to tell her that she was sorry. I thought she meant for stealing the necklace, but now it's a mystery."

"We'll probably never know what happened," he agreed. "Does it really matter? Look at the other photos in that album. They were best friends once, and because of that, now you and I are friends too."

Something in the tone of his voice caused Kaydi to meet his eyes. She saw more than friendship in his gaze. "I'm glad we're not related."

"I am too." Luke reached for her hand. "Do you still want to go out for pizza?"

"Absolutely." Kaydi glanced down at the photo album. "Do you think I could get copies of these photos while we're in town?"

"The album is yours."

"No, I couldn't take it."

"Please do. I got out the Bible again. After the listings of births are marriages and deaths. Even though they were so far apart in age, I'm fairly certain Caroline was Jedidiah's sister. She never married, and she died fairly young. No matter what happened between Caroline and your grandma—if anything ever did—I think it's only fitting that the album go to you."

"Thank you." Kaydi hugged the album to her chest. "This means so much to me. To get to know my grandmother as she was when she was about my age. That's priceless."

"Maybe one of the photos will give you a clue about where your grandmother lived," he said. "Who her people are."

"I'll be studying every single one."

Luke stood and held out his hand. "You can do that later. Right now, the sun is shining, the birds are singing, and the water is fine. How about going out on the boat with me? We'll motor over to the town dock and get that pizza."

"What if I get sick again?" she asked.

"You need to find your sea legs if we're going to—you know."

"You know what?"

"We'll talk about that later."

Kaydi's heart raced at his unspoken words. "I need to get my Life Savers."

"That's my girl."

Kaydi spontaneously kissed him on the cheek.

Luke immediately put his arm around her waist and drew her close. "I've never met anyone quite like you, Kaydi-Paris Alexandria Engstrom. I don't want you to go."

Had he said what she thought he said? She wasn't sure she wanted to leave either. How ridiculous would it be to uproot her entire life for someone she'd just met a few days ago? Yet she felt connected to Luke and this place in a way she'd never felt before. Family and friends often chided her for her impulsive notions, but those impulses had never led her astray. She didn't think they would now.

"Any chance you'd come to Omaha?" she asked.

"Wherever you are, that's where I want to be."

"You have strong roots here," Kaydi reminded him. "Deep roots."

"It'll always be home, but it doesn't have to be my only home." Luke cleared his throat, then gazed deep into her eyes. "I hope it doesn't have to be *our* only home."

Again, the unspoken words flew between them, warming Kaydi's cheeks and speeding up her heart. There was no use denying the truth any longer.

She was falling in love.

She'd carry a roll of butter rum Life Savers the rest of her life if she had to.

Grace

Grace set the tray of appetizers in the middle of Spencer's dining room table along with a small stack of plates and folded napkins.

"They're here." Spencer entered from the foyer and eyed the table. "That's a lot of food. I hope you're not disappointed if there are plenty of leftovers. They didn't come to eat."

Grace shrugged. "Food can be relaxing. Besides, I had to do something to keep from being a wreck myself."

"Why are you nervous?" he asked.

"I'm worried about Danielle and her mystery guy. What if he's guilty and playing on her sympathies? I'm not sure I like him."

The doorbell rang, and Spencer gave her a reassuring smile. "Let's greet our guests."

They walked together past the kitchen to the foyer.

Spencer opened the door. "Please come in."

Danielle entered first. She appeared pale, and her nervous smile almost broke Grace's heart. All she could do now was pray that Spencer could help her.

"I'm Spencer Lewis." He extended his hand.

"Thank you for seeing us," the man said before entering.

Grace widened her eyes at the familiar voice. "Clayton Lowe? You're Danielle's mystery man?"

He held out his hands. "Guilty. How's Winston?"

"No longer smelling like a skunk," Grace answered. "That recipe you found worked wonders."

Clayton smiled. "I'm glad."

"Why didn't you tell me?" Grace glanced from Danielle to Clayton. "You're an accountant? Why are you called Ace?"

The others laughed at Grace's barrage of questions.

Clayton raised his hands. "Oliver Nichols is my cousin. When I came here, he added me to his crew to keep me from sitting around the house and going crazy."

"I never would have guessed," Grace said. "You've done a great job with our lawn."

"I worked in the business during the summers when I was a teen," Clayton explained. "That was before our uncle turned Two Green Thumbs over to Oliver."

"Ace is my nickname for him," Danielle added. "It's just a silly joke that started when we first met."

"And because Clayton came to Magnolia Harbor, you did too," Grace said.

"It had been a long time since I prayed," Danielle replied. "Like I told you before, when Ace said he had a cousin in Magnolia Harbor, it seemed like God was leading me to you."

"I'm sure He was," Grace said. "I'm glad."

"Let's go into the dining room," Spencer suggested as he gestured toward the table. "Grace fixed us plenty of refreshments."

Danielle laughed, seeming to be at ease for the first time since she entered the house. "Of course she did. There's no one more hospitable."

"Food makes everything better," Grace said as she directed them to their seats.

Once they were settled with drinks and snacks, Spencer opened a notepad and took the cap off his ballpoint pen.

"You're taking notes?" Danielle asked. She sounded skeptical.

"The old-fashioned way." Spencer gave her a reassuring smile.

"No one will see them but me, and I'll shred them once this is over. You have my word."

"I guess that's okay then," Danielle said.

"Who wants to start?" Spencer asked.

"I will," Clayton volunteered. "It was supposed to be a simple sweepstakes promotion designed to get people to come to the restaurants." He continued with the details of the sweepstakes and the evidence of bribery with Danielle filling in the gaps.

When they finished, no one said anything for a few moments.

Spencer capped his pen and closed the notepad. "I have a friend who'll be interested in your story. He'll know the best way to expose the true felons in this case."

"What about Ace?" Danielle asked. Her voice sounded weak and tired.

Grace could tell it had been all Danielle could do to keep it together as she and Clayton had talked about their fears of being blamed for the theft of the winning tickets.

"For now, my best advice is to keep doing what you're doing." The reassuring tone in Spencer's voice comforted Grace. She hoped it did the same for Danielle and Clayton. "As soon as I've talked to my contact, I'll be in touch with you."

"Will Ace have to give himself up?" Danielle asked.

"Probably," Spencer said. "But not until we learn more about what we're up against. Even then, I'd suggest you talk to an attorney before contacting anyone at the restaurant. I'll try to reach my guy today, so hopefully this ordeal won't go on much longer."

"Please know that we support you and want to do everything we can to help," Grace said.

"That's kind of you." Danielle placed her napkin beside her plate. "I'm glad there was an opening at the inn the day I arrived."

"So am I," Grace said with a smile.

"I guess we should be going now," Clayton said. "We're going fishing."

"Fishing?" Grace echoed, glancing at Danielle.

She laughed. "We're starting a new tradition. Friday afternoon fishing."

"It's a first for both of us, but Oliver gave me a few tips." Clayton scooted his chair back from the table, stood, and extended his hand to Spencer. "Thank you for your help. I'm still not sure I'll come out of this with my reputation intact, but you've given me hope."

Spencer stood, and the two men shook hands. "I'll do everything possible for you."

Danielle and Grace also rose, and Danielle gave Grace a hug.

After Danielle and Clayton left, Grace went to work clearing the table and placing the leftovers in containers. When Spencer offered to help, she shooed him away to make his phone call.

The call needed to be made, but that wasn't the only reason she'd refused his assistance. It was nice being in his home again, puttering around his kitchen as she'd done on so many other occasions when she'd helped with his dinner parties and get-togethers. She enjoyed the familiarity of the space and the warm memories evoked by being here.

She needed to be alone for a few minutes. More precisely, she needed for Spencer not to be so close to her for a few minutes. Their friendship was slowly getting back on track, but there were still moments when . . .

Grace didn't allow herself to finish her train of thought. She snapped the lid shut on the container of cookies and blinked away a tear.

26

Kaydi

Kaydi practically floated up the stairs as she headed for the Wisteria Loft Suite to change clothes and grab her Life Savers. She couldn't believe she was this excited about going out on Luke's boat again, but everything had changed since finding out that she and Luke weren't related.

Since finding out he was falling in love with her, as she was with him.

She wanted to squeal with delight, sing at the top of her lungs, and dance a pirouette while tossing flowers all around.

Her parents would say it was too soon and everything was happening way too fast. Deep in her heart, Kaydi knew her impracticality wasn't an impulsive whim. What she felt for Luke was unlike anything she'd ever felt before. She was falling in love with him. Time wouldn't change the depth of her feelings for this wonderful, creative, funny, considerate man.

When she got to her room, she quickly changed into shorts and a tank top, then swiped on sunscreen. The Life Savers were in her bag, but where was her phone? She glanced around the room and spotted it on the dresser.

As soon as the phone was in her hand, the screen lit up and showed a missed call and a voice mail notification.

Julep Buckley's name appeared on the screen. She had finally answered Kaydi's call.

She sat on the edge of the chair by the fireplace and tapped the screen to access her voice mail.

"This is Julep Buckley," an elderly woman said. "I'm sorry I missed your call, but I've been away from home. I'm back now and staying put for the rest of the day. If you'd still like to have a chat, then ring me up again. Have a nice day now."

Enchanted by Julep's sweet Southern charm even in a voice mail to a stranger, Kaydi listened to the message again.

What should she do?

She'd already found out that her grandmother and Caroline had been best friends. Unfortunately, nothing in the photo album Luke had found gave any clues to where the Emmett family had lived. Kaydi supposed they might have lived somewhere else. Perhaps her grandma had often stayed at Foxsong Meadows because of her friendship with Caroline.

If that was true, Kaydi might never know any more about her grandmother's family. Or her grandfather's. She needed to study the album to see if anyone in the photos resembled her grandfather. If so, maybe she'd be able to prove or disprove her theory that socialite Callie Jo Emmett had eloped with the gardener's son.

Returning to the newspaper archives and the library's microfiche didn't appeal to Kaydi at all, but she should talk to Julep before she returned to Omaha. Even if the woman knew nothing of her grandparents, at least Kaydi would have done her best.

Besides, returning the call was the polite thing to do. Proper etiquette wasn't only proper in the South. Midwesterners had good manners as well.

Kaydi took a deep breath and made the call.

Julep answered on the third ring.

"This is Kaydi Engstrom. I'm staying at the Magnolia Harbor Inn, and Winnie Bennett gave me your number."

"A friend of Winnie's, are you?" Julep laughed. "Well, it's always a delight to meet friends of my friends. Especially when their voices are as young and sweet-sounding as yours."

Flustered by the unexpected compliment, Kaydi took a moment to reply. "Thank you." She was eager to visit Julep as soon as possible, but she couldn't pinpoint the reason for her inexplicable urgency.

"I'm so glad you called me again," Julep said. "What can I do for you?"

"I came to town to see if I could find out something about my grandmother," Kaydi said. "She talked about Foxsong Meadows before she died. I think she might have either lived around here or at least spent time here when she was young."

"I'm so sorry for your loss." Julep's voice was sympathetic. "What was your grandmother's name?"

"Her maiden name was Callie Jo Emmett," Kaydi answered. "My grandfather was Joseph Piper."

The line was silent for a moment. Was Julep remembering something about Kaydi's grandparents?

"Those names aren't familiar to me," Julep finally said. "If you're wanting to know more about Foxsong Meadows, you should talk to Luke Brannick. That place has been in his family for several generations now."

Kaydi smiled to herself. "I know Luke."

"Oh?" Julep asked. Apparently, the older woman had picked up on the warmth in Kaydi's voice when she'd said Luke's name.

"We found a photo album belonging to Luke's great-grandfather's sister. Her name was Caroline, though my grandmother called her Carrie Anne. The album has the names 'Callie Jo and Carrie Anne' printed on the front."

"You don't say! I'd like to see that album. That is, if you and Luke don't mind sharing it with me."

"We'd love to," Kaydi said honestly.

Before she could ask Julep for a convenient time, the older woman spoke. "How soon can you get here?"

"We're both at the inn right now." Kaydi thought quickly. "Fifteen minutes, maybe? Is that too soon?"

"That's just right," Julep said. "So Luke is with you? Well, if that don't beat all."

"Ma'am?" Kaydi asked. What did Julep mean by that?

"Never mind the musings of an old woman." Julep chuckled. "Now get yourselves over here quick as you can. I'm waiting for you."

Kaydi promised they'd be there soon and ended the call. She sat for a moment longer, replaying the unusual phone call while appreciating Julep's kindness and warmth and wondering why Julep had chuckled over Luke. What was that all about?

She'd know soon enough.

A change of plans meant a change of clothes and no boat ride. Even with the butter rum Life Savers, Kaydi didn't plan to arrive at Julep's house with even the slightest hint of seasickness. She'd drive them to Julep's, and Luke could come back for his boat later.

Maybe he'd suggest a moonlit cruise on the lake. How romantic would that be?

She'd save her Life Savers for that possibility.

Luke didn't seem to mind the change of plans. "You're going to love Julep," he'd said when Kaydi told him about the phone call.

She already did, though she was nervous about meeting her. Since Julep lived on Lake Haven Road, only about half a mile from the inn, they arrived at the brick Colonial-style house in only a few minutes.

If not for the afternoon heat, they could have walked.

Kaydi parked her car, and Luke took her arm as they strolled along the path, edged with blooming azaleas, that led to brick steps and a screened-in porch.

Julep welcomed them at the door, and Luke bent to kiss her cheek before introducing her to Kaydi.

"Aren't you a pretty thing?" Julep exclaimed. "I knew you would be by the sound of your voice. Come and sit. I have sweet tea and a few little treats on that tray over there. Luke, you can serve if you don't mind while I get acquainted with your young lady."

"Yes ma'am," Luke said. He smiled at Kaydi. "I plead the fifth on any stories she tells you about me."

Julep playfully swatted his arm. "We'll let bygones be bygones," she teased. "You're a fine young man now that you've found your place in this world." She turned to Kaydi. "I suppose you've seen his art."

"A few pieces, yes."

"I don't always understand their meaning," Julep said. "But I do know talent when I see it." She guided Kaydi to a sofa situated between cushioned wicker chairs.

The screened porch exuded the feel of an indoor garden with its comfortable furniture, multiple flowering plants, and a couple of palms potted in huge baskets.

"Now sit down and tell me all about yourself." Julep sat in an adjacent chair.

Kaydi told Julep about her family, growing up in Omaha, and her business selling reclaimed vintage jewelry and her own redesigned pieces on online shopping sites.

Meanwhile, Luke poured tea into tall glasses of ice and added lemon slices and sprigs of mint. He delivered the glasses, then served brownies with strawberries.

After chatting for a few more minutes, Julep set her plate on the round glass table beside her chair. "Did you bring the photo album?"

"I have it right here." Kaydi removed the album from her bag and handed it to Julep.

The older woman read the inscription on the front, and a small smile lifted her thin lips. "I've been thinking about Caroline ever since you called." She gently ran her fingers over the cover.

"You knew her?" Luke asked.

"Not well. She wasn't a happy woman, I'm sorry to say. She was only in her early forties when she died."

Julep's words sent a tinge of unease up Kaydi's spine. She wanted to ask Julep if she knew why Caroline wasn't happy, but she was afraid of the answer. What if her sadness had something to do with Kaydi's grandmother?

Kaydi closed her eyes against the anxiety building within her, wishing she understood its cause. Whatever happened between her grandma and Caroline had happened a long time ago. Perhaps it wasn't something she should dig up.

Yet another part of her needed to know her ancestry. Who was her grandmother? Who were the Emmetts and the Pipers? Where had they come from, and when had they lived in Magnolia Harbor?

"Do you remember my grandma?" Kaydi asked Julep, her voice small and hesitant.

Instead of answering, Julep perused the pages of the album. She seemed to be scrutinizing each photo.

Kaydi wondered if the pictures were helping Julep remember the olden days of debutante balls and cotillions. When young women wore broad hats and carried parasols against the summer heat. When they went on shopping trips to Charleston and Savannah and Atlanta. Kaydi imagined a Southern charm that was often found only in close-knit towns like Magnolia Harbor.

"It happened so long ago," Julep said. "I was young enough that I suppose my parents tried to hide the story from me."

Story? Kaydi leaned forward and realized she was crumpling her napkin in her fist.

Julep smiled at Kaydi, but her eyes were pensive, almost sad. "I don't know all the details, so I'm hesitant to say anything. I could be mistaken."

"You don't think you are," Luke said. "Do you?"

Julep shook her head. "There were whispers. Children are attracted to whispers and secrets."

Luke placed his hand on Julep's arm. "Tell us what you heard."

"Are you sure you want to know?" Julep asked Kaydi.

"I do," she answered. Whatever Julep had to say couldn't be as bad as not knowing the truth. Besides, wasn't this why she had hopped on a plane all by herself and traveled halfway across the country? "Please tell me."

"As I remember them, Caroline—her friends called her Carrie Anne back then—and Callie Jo were practically inseparable," Julep began. "They'd been friends since they were children, but not everyone thought the friendship should be allowed."

"Why not?" Kaydi asked.

"It was a different time," Julep explained. "The social classes were more defined. There were those who thought a girl should stay in the class she was born into instead of having ideas about being more than she should expect to be."

"You mean my grandma?" Kaydi asked. She'd built up such expectations in her own imagination. She didn't mind that her grandmother wasn't what she expected her to be, but she couldn't help feeling a tiny bit disappointed. "Her family wasn't wealthy?"

"Like I said, the details are fuzzy," Julep replied. "I believe Callie Jo's mother was the housekeeper at Foxsong Meadows."

"I didn't think housekeepers had children," Luke said.

"Most didn't, but some did. Callie Jo's father probably worked on the estate too. Maybe in the stables or the fields."

"I have a census record saying my grandfather's father worked as a gardener," Kaydi said. "It doesn't say where, but maybe he worked at Foxsong Meadows. Maybe that's how my grandparents met."

"Sounds plausible," Julep said. She tilted her head as if lost in thought. "Yes, that was part of the story."

"What was?" Kaydi asked.

"They ran away together. The gardener's son and the housekeeper's daughter." Julep's voice rose in excitement as the memory seemed to be coming back to her. "It was quite the scandal. And even more so because the elopement left Caroline brokenhearted."

"She was mad because my grandma left her?" Kaydi didn't want to believe that. In the photos, her grandmother and Caroline always appeared happy together, as if they were the best of friends. Why wouldn't Caroline be pleased for her?

"Caroline was in love with the gardener's son too," Julep said. "Of course, she was forbidden to have anything to do with him once her affections were known, but that didn't stop her from feeling betrayed when he turned his attentions to the friend who was like a sister to her."

"They were so much in love," Kaydi said. "My grandparents, I mean. It's hard to believe he ever loved someone else."

"He may not have been in love with Caroline," Julep said. "I guess we'll never know for sure. Only that she loved him and that he left to build a different kind of life with Callie Jo. A life that eventually meant you were born. And now here you are." Julep glanced slyly at Luke. "Finding your own friends in our small town."

Luke took Kaydi's hand. "I'm glad your grandma eloped with the gardener's son, and I'm glad you came here to find out more about your family."

"Me too." Kaydi squeezed his hand. "But I'm sorry for Caroline. She must have been so hurt. It sounds like she never got over it."

"I don't believe she ever married," Julep said.

"She didn't," Luke replied. "At least, there's no marriage listed in the family Bible."

"You have a tender heart, Kaydi," Julep said kindly. "We all have our heartbreaks, our own set of troubles. We all choose how we'll respond to them. Unfortunately, Caroline decided to shut herself away instead of giving love—or even friendship—another chance."

"It might have been the first time in her life when things didn't work out the way she wanted them to," Luke said. "That can be difficult to deal with."

"You may be right," Julep said. "Caroline led the pampered life of a Southern belle in a different era. From these photos, I'd say she truly loved Callie Jo and considered her an equal, not a servant."

Kaydi sat back with a sigh. "There's so much I wish I could ask my grandmother. It would have been such fun to show her this photo album."

Luke put his arm around her, and she leaned into him. When she'd first started planning this trip, she'd hoped to find a family branch that she hadn't met before. She'd hoped to fill in the gaps in her grandmother's memories. Instead, she'd found how love had brought two people together while breaking the heart of a dear friend.

Love had also touched her heart.

"I'm glad Winnie suggested you call me," Julep said. "Thinking about Caroline and seeing these photographs has led me to recall my own debutante years. Oh, we had some wonderful times, my friends and I. Such glorious memories. I suppose I never expected my world to be anything but joyful back then." She gazed fondly at Luke and Kaydi. "Would you like to hear how I met my husband?"

"I would love that," Kaydi said.

For the next hour or so, Kaydi and Luke listened to Julep's stories about her courtship and wedding, about her life as a young wife and mother. What a delightful woman she was. In a way, Julep reminded Kaydi of her grandmother.

That wasn't really a surprise. Even though her grandma had been the housekeeper's daughter, she'd participated in many events with her friend that were usually reserved for the upper classes. Like Julep, her grandmother had been a gracious hostess with high standards of etiquette and the poise of a lady.

The time passed quickly as the three laughed and talked together.

When it came time to leave, Luke volunteered to take the dishes into the kitchen.

Julep thanked him, then moved to the couch to sit beside Kaydi. "I know I said this already, but I am very happy you called."

"I'm glad we were able to meet," Kaydi responded. "Thank you for solving the mystery of my family."

"Remember what I told you," Julep warned. "I may not have all the details right."

"I think you have the broad picture," Kaydi said. "I'm going home knowing more about my grandma than I did when I left. That means the world to me."

"What about Luke?" Julep's eyes twinkled with mischief. "I think he means something too."

Though Kaydi blushed, she couldn't help being pleased with Julep's unabashed curiosity. She'd never have the chance to tell her grandmother about the man she'd met on her impromptu trip to Magnolia Harbor, but she believed she could safely confide in this dear woman who'd shown such hospitality and warmth to a stranger.

"He does," she said softly. "I've never met anyone like him."

"I've known Luke all his life," Julep said. "He's had his troubles, especially after his father died, but he found his way again and grew into a fine young man. I've been praying he'd meet the perfect woman for him. Perhaps God has finally answered my prayers."

"I'm far from perfect," Kaydi said with a laugh.

Julep tapped Kaydi's arm. "I said perfect for Luke. There's a difference."

"What's a difference?" Luke asked as he returned to the porch.

"Never you mind." Julep handed the photo album to Kaydi. "You two have made my day, but Missy Perkins called just before you arrived about a meeting at the chamber of commerce. It's apparently my duty to attend. Kaydi, will I see you at church on Sunday?"

"I'd love to be there, but my flight leaves from Charleston that morning."

"We don't want to talk about that," Luke put in. "Time is going too fast."

"Then I advise you to enjoy every minute you have together," Julep said as she walked them to the porch door.

Both Kaydi and Luke gave the older woman a hug as they said their goodbyes.

As they walked to the rental car, Luke caught Kaydi's hand.

She'd been trying to avoid thinking about her return flight until Julep brought up church. In only two days, she'd be on a plane to Omaha. How long would it be until she saw Luke again? Hopefully she could take Julep's advice and enjoy every minute with him.

She tried to ignore how the thought of leaving him caused her heart to ache.

27

Luke

Kaydi was leaving Sunday morning, so Luke didn't have much time. He reflected on her imminent departure from the time they left Julep's house and all through their dinner at Cappy's.

After supper, they sat together for hours in the music room at the inn and talked about the past and the present—everything except the future. He couldn't let Kaydi fly back to Omaha without knowing if she felt the same way about him as he did about her.

When it was time for Luke to go home, Kaydi walked him to the dock. The full moon bathed them in soft light as they embraced. She fit so neatly into his arms, and he placed a kiss on her soft cheek. She wrapped her arms around his neck and pressed her sweet lips against his.

He could have stood on the dock all night holding her close.

Eventually they said a reluctant goodbye, and Luke motored toward the marina in Magnolia Harbor.

As he was riding to Foxsong Meadows on his motorcycle, he considered everything Julep had told him about Caroline. Suddenly, a memory surfaced.

After he'd read *Treasure Island* and become obsessed with maps and hidden treasure, his grandmother had told him about an old maple along the fence that was rumored to have been used as a hiding place for secret messages. She wasn't sure exactly which tree since there were several that separated the cultivated lawn from the woods on the other side of the fence. She wasn't even sure if the story was true.

Luke had been ten or eleven at the time. Just the suggestion of a message tree had ignited his imagination, and he'd spent an adventurous afternoon searching for the hiding place. Eventually he'd found a hole near the split in the trunk of one of the trees. The hole was lined with scraps of metal that had been soldered together to form a type of box.

But Luke's dream of finding a hidden treasure map had been dashed. There was nothing inside the hole except for a few stray pieces of lilac stationery. Any words that had been written on the pages had faded to almost nothing. But it didn't matter. Everyone knew pirates didn't use lilac stationery for treasure maps.

What mattered was the hiding place.

Luke and his friends had left messages for one another in the tree throughout that summer, drawing their own maps that led to secret caches where they'd hidden cookies, polished stones, and oddities treasured by young boys.

He hadn't thought of the old maple or the lilac stationery in years, but in light of what Julep had said, he wondered if it was possible the note had been written by Callie Jo and intended for the gardener's son.

Or had it been written by Caroline, who might have thought Joseph's heart belonged to her until he eloped with her best friend?

Unfortunately, that mystery would never be solved. The answer was in the past, lost to them forever.

Nevertheless, Kaydi needed to see the tree before she went home. They'd already made plans to meet Clint at Aunt Patsy's Porch for breakfast. Maybe they could come back here afterward.

Luke's mind whirled with possibilities. Maybe he could leave a present for Kaydi in the tree. Something to remember him by. Something that would let her know how important she was to him.

Something to let her know he loved her. Because as ridiculous as it was to feel that way after knowing her less than a week, he was certain that was what this was.

As soon as he got home, Luke went straight to his bedroom and pushed a button behind the framed painting of Timber, the prized stallion that had once given Foxsong Meadows popular renown among the horse-racing set. Unfortunately, the horse had to be auctioned off to pay the gambling debts of an ancestor, and the Foxsong Meadows stables never achieved their previous fame again. Luke still liked the painting, though. Besides, it served another purpose.

The frame slid to the side, revealing an old-fashioned safe that had been built into the wall. Luke rotated the knob, entering the combination to the safe. A click sounded, and he opened the safe.

The interior of the safe was about the size of a large safety deposit box. Among other things, it held Luke's passport, a few hundred dollars in cash—a habit instilled in him by his father, who'd believed easy access to money was a safeguard against emergencies such as hurricanes—and a few other legal documents.

Several jewelry boxes also took up space. Luke pulled out a few of these until he finally found the piece he wanted. If he remembered correctly, the ring had belonged to his great-grandmother on his father's side. Gold filigree surrounded an oval amethyst nestled in diamonds. His mother, who preferred a diamond solitaire set in a white-gold band, thought it was gaudy.

Kaydi, with her bohemian aesthetic, would love it.

At least, Luke hoped she would.

Besides, this ring was temporary. If Kaydi said yes, they'd go shopping together so she could choose the ring she wanted.

Luke returned the ring to its box and closed the safe. The painting of Timber slid back into place.

Luke knew that his family and friends would tell him that he was rushing things. That to marry in haste meant repenting in leisure. He couldn't totally dismiss the truth in the old saying, nor the concerns of those who cared about him.

Deep inside his gut, Luke was certain that there was no one for him except the gorgeous woman with the dusting of freckles on her nose who'd turned his head at the Norwood estate sale. He wasn't making this decision from fear of her leaving. No, it was because of his hope that they'd travel together—literally, as in back to her home in Omaha, and figuratively, that they'd walk the same path into the future.

He went to sleep with the jewelry box beneath his pillow and dreamed of sitting with Kaydi on the dilapidated mansion's veranda while their grandchildren played on the front lawn.

28

Grace

Jack and Melissa were the only guests at breakfast on Saturday morning, and Grace and Charlotte had joined them for the meal. Chet and Mandy and their boys had left the day before, Kaydi was meeting Luke at the diner, and Danielle had driven away about the same time.

As soon as Jack and Melissa finished their meal, they left to begin their long drive home to Michigan.

After Grace and Winston saw them off, they went to the kitchen. Grace poured herself another cup of coffee, and Winston bounded over to Charlotte.

She reached down to scratch behind the dog's ears, then asked her sister, "What's on your agenda for the day?"

"Cleaning the unoccupied suites," Grace replied. "Mandy brought down all their towels before she left. I always tell her she doesn't have to do that, but she does it anyway."

"Our regular guests become more like family, don't they?" Charlotte added plates to the dishwasher. "I wish they could have stayed through the weekend."

"So do I."

"I'm sorry I wasn't here to see them off," Charlotte said. "At least I got a chance to say goodbye before I went to Hanson's." Hanson's Farm Fresh Foods was one of Charlotte's favorite places to shop for fresh fruits and veggies to inspire her menus.

"Robbie and Henry loved the bags of treats you made for them,"

Grace said. "They wanted to open them right away, but Mandy told them they had to wait until they'd been on the road for a while."

"They're such sweet boys," Charlotte said as she started putting the leftover muffins in an airtight container. "I always love having them here."

Grace absentmindedly nodded. She almost hadn't made it back to the inn before the Zemas needed to leave because she had been at Spencer's house with Danielle and Clayton. Winnie had been kind enough to stay at the inn while both Grace and Charlotte were gone.

Charlotte suddenly stopped what she was doing and raised an eyebrow. "What's wrong?"

Grace startled. "Nothing."

"Then why do I feel like you're a hundred miles away instead of in this room with me?"

"I'm right here," Grace said, trying to put as much reassurance into her voice as she could. So far, she had avoided talking to Charlotte about Danielle's problems, but she didn't like keeping secrets from her sister.

"You never told me why that man from Maddox Creative called."

"No, I didn't," Grace said. "I can't."

"Why not?" Charlotte asked. She could be so persistent.

Perhaps Charlotte had a right to know since the situation involved one of their guests. But Danielle would never trust Grace again if she told Charlotte what was going on.

"Does this have anything to do with your mysterious meeting at my cottage?" Charlotte pressed.

"Please don't ask me."

Charlotte huffed, then put away the rest of the muffins. "Winnie said you were at Spencer's yesterday. How is he doing?"

Her innocent tone and feigned indifference didn't fool Grace.

Charlotte had been almost as upset at Hank's sudden reappearance as Grace. She'd been as supportive as possible, but she also wanted Grace and Spencer to be a couple.

Maybe—someday—they would be. Or maybe it was too late, and they'd only ever be friends. Grace was okay with that.

Most of the time.

"Aren't you going to answer me?" Charlotte asked.

"I'm sorry. What did you say?"

"I asked about Spencer. How is he doing?"

"Fine. He went on a trip with his daughters, and they had a good time." Grace took a sip of her coffee, then set the cup on the counter. She no longer wanted it. "I'm going upstairs to get started on the rooms."

"I'll help you once I finish up here," Charlotte offered.

"No need," Grace said. "I think the activity will do me good."

"You mean it will keep your mind off things you don't want to think about."

"Perhaps I do."

Charlotte frowned. "I'm sorry. I shouldn't have been so blunt. You've just seemed so preoccupied. And then you got that message, and I'm worried about you."

"Please don't be." Grace rounded the island and gave her sister a hug. "I'm fine. Or at least I will be."

Charlotte started to reply, but she was interrupted by a knock on the kitchen door.

Winston jumped up and barked.

The door opened, and Danielle entered followed by Clayton. Instead of his Two Green Thumbs uniform, he wore blue shorts with a cream polo.

Winston warmly greeted them.

"Mind if we come in?" Danielle asked.

"Of course not. Have a seat." Grace gestured to the stools at the island. "Would you like some coffee?"

Charlotte glanced at Grace, who easily interpreted the question in her sister's eyes. *Danielle and Oliver's cousin? What's up with that?*

Grace ignored her. "We have muffins and fruit too," she offered.

"That sounds wonderful," Danielle said, "but we don't want to be any trouble."

"No trouble at all," Charlotte said with a smile. She immediately pushed the container of muffins toward them.

Grace poured the coffee. She couldn't blame her sister for being curious. So was she. For the first time since Danielle had arrived, she appeared happy. The tension was gone from around her eyes, and her movements were relaxed. If Grace wasn't mistaken, Danielle also had that special glow of a woman in love.

Clayton, or Ace as Danielle called him, also appeared at ease. He shifted his stool closer to Danielle's, one of those natural but often unconscious gestures that indicated closeness.

Grace set two cups of coffee and a small pitcher of creamer on the island.

"We wanted to give you an update," Clayton said as he added creamer to his cup.

Charlotte placed plates in front of them along with a bowl of fruit salad. "I can start on the rooms and give you some privacy."

Danielle glanced at Grace in surprise. "She doesn't know?"

"It was your secret to tell," Grace said. "Not mine."

Danielle smiled her thanks, then turned to Charlotte. "Please stay. We can't thank Grace enough for everything she's done for us."

"We met with Spencer again last night," Clayton said. "His FBI friend was interested in our story. We're not in the clear yet, but he was very encouraging."

At the mention of the FBI, Charlotte widened her eyes.

"I'd like to stay at the inn a little longer," Danielle said. "That is, if you still have an available room."

"Of course. I can move you to the Wisteria Loft Suite after Kaydi checks out tomorrow," Grace said. "It's on the third floor."

"Perfect," Danielle said. "You don't know how much your hospitality means to me, Grace. And your friendship."

"I'm glad I could help," Grace said. "Though I didn't really do that much."

"You believed in me," Danielle said, then took Clayton's hand. "You believed in us. Hopefully, this nightmare will soon be over."

"Nightmare?" Charlotte echoed. "FBI? No more secrets. Tell me what's going on."

Clayton held up his free hand. "Allow me," he said with a smile. "First, even though I worked my way through college doing landscaping jobs, I'm actually an accountant. Oliver Nichols is my cousin. When I needed a place to hide, he and Elaina graciously took me in and put me on his crew."

"I always thought you were more the white-collar type," Charlotte said.

Grace understood what her sister meant. She'd thought the same thing.

"I do prefer working with numbers to mowing and mulching," he admitted.

"Or returning a skunk-soaked dog to his owner?" Grace made a face at the memory.

"I definitely prefer spreadsheets to that," Clayton said.

They all laughed.

Clayton quickly brought Charlotte up to speed on how he and Danielle were suspected by their respective companies of stealing the winning sweepstakes tickets.

"Grace introduced us to Spencer," Danielle explained. "Then Spencer introduced us to a former colleague who specializes in these kinds of crimes. We spent hours last night going through our stories and the documentation that Clayton had."

"We met with him again this morning for breakfast." Clayton selected a muffin from the basket. "He recommended a lawyer in Charleston for us to talk to while he completes his investigation. Since neither my firm nor Maddox Creative will want the bad publicity which could come from a full-scale investigation, he believes they'll cooperate in flushing out the perpetrators so our names will be cleared."

"We're meeting with the attorney this afternoon." Danielle shivered. "I'm still afraid of going back to Charleston, so we're meeting her at Two Green Thumbs among the fertilizer and grass seed."

Clayton gently elbowed her. "It's not that bad. Oliver is letting us use his office, which isn't much bigger than a broom closet."

"You could meet here," Grace said.

"Or at my cottage," Charlotte volunteered.

Danielle smiled at the two sisters. "You're both very kind, but we've imposed on your hospitality too much already. Besides, I want to see where Ace works."

"I keep telling her there isn't much to see, but she insists." Clayton's tone sounded annoyed, but the teasing look in his eyes as he gazed at Danielle said quite the opposite.

"You won't be there much longer, so I have to check it out while I can," Danielle playfully answered.

"You're not going back to the restaurant chain, are you?" Grace asked, then waved her hand as if to erase the words she'd just said. "I'm sorry for being so nosy."

"There's no need to apologize," Clayton assured her. He grinned at Danielle. "You tell them."

Danielle took a deep breath as if to gather her thoughts. A broad smile lit up her face. "We're starting our own business." She squealed as if she were a young girl announcing her first job.

Grace couldn't help but laugh. This was a side of Danielle she'd never seen before. "What kind of business?"

"A boutique marketing firm providing individualized services to a select clientele," Danielle answered. "I'll handle the creative side, and Ace will take care of the day-to-day business details."

"Won't you have to leave Charleston?" Grace had signed a noncompete agreement when she resigned from the VP position at Maddox Creative. No doubt Danielle would have to do the same.

"We will, but we're going to relocate," Danielle said. "Both of us."

"A new adventure in a new state," Clayton added.

"You're not even staying in South Carolina?" Charlotte asked. Her tone made it clear what she thought of that idea.

Grace refrained from rolling her eyes. Her sister definitely believed the Palmetto State was the best of all the states. She'd never consider moving somewhere else. To be honest, Grace wouldn't either. Both of them had lived in South Carolina all their lives. Their roots were sunk deep into the low country, and those roots had grown especially strong here in Magnolia Harbor since they'd bought the inn.

"We're thinking of going out west," Clayton said. "Maybe Montana."

"We might even raise a few head of cattle." Danielle snickered. "Can you see me roping a calf, Grace?"

"I think you can do anything you set your mind to." Grace smiled. "I mean that."

They continued to chat, and then Grace excused herself to clean the empty suites. As she ascended the stairs, her heart was lighter than it had been earlier. She hadn't realized the intensity of the burden she'd felt for Danielle and Clayton until it had been lifted. Not only that, it warmed her heart to see the obvious affection the two had for each other.

That warmth also soothed her spirit and led her to a spontaneous prayer of gratitude. *Thank You, Father, that I can be happy for my friends without feeling sorry for myself. Talking to Spencer was awkward, but as we came together to help others, we somehow found our footing again.*

We can be good friends—even close friends—and if the future holds something more for us, so be it. For now, I'm content.

Truly content.

29

Kaydi

The motorcycle ride from Aunt Patsy's Porch to Foxsong Meadows thrilled Kaydi from the top of her tousled head to her pedicured toes. She met Clint, and she liked him from the get-go. The head waitress, Molly, had greeted her as if she were a long-lost relative who had finally come home.

The other diners didn't bother to hide their curiosity when she and Luke had entered hand in hand. They all wanted to meet "the pretty stranger who finally captured our Luke's heart" as one elderly matron worded it. Lottie Duprie was a retired schoolteacher who'd taught Luke when he was a "gangly young man."

Clint and Molly had finally run interference and got the couple seated in a booth where they could enjoy their breakfast. Even then, more than one person stopped to say hello on their way out the door. Kaydi couldn't recall a time when she'd received such a warm welcome. In only a few days, she'd fallen in love with the small-town charm of Magnolia Harbor—and with one particular resident.

Kaydi laughed as she took off her helmet after Luke had parked the motorcycle beside his gatehouse.

"This has been the most wonderful week," she said. "I can't believe all the things I've done in just a few days. Flying, boating, motorcycling. I'm only sorry we never made it to the lighthouse."

Though maybe she shouldn't push her luck. Would the butter rum Life Savers ease her fear of heights as they had her seasickness? Who knew? Somehow, she didn't mind finding out—especially if Luke was by her side.

"It's not too late." Luke took the helmet from her, then wrapped his arms around her waist. "We have the entire day ahead of us. It'll take a couple of hours to get there, but we can climb the lighthouse, stroll along the beach, and find a quiet spot for dinner."

How could Kaydi say no to such a romantic day? A wave of sadness swept over her as she realized this could be her last full day with Luke. She stifled a sigh and pushed the feeling away. Today was a day for smiles, for making a treasured memory. She'd have enough time for sadness when she woke up in the morning. When she turned in her rental car. When she boarded the plane. Each step would take her farther from the man she'd fallen for so quickly and completely.

She closed her eyes and mentally shook away her dread.

"You don't want to go?" Luke asked. He sounded hurt.

She gazed into his eyes and rested her palm against his cheek. "There's nothing else I'd rather do."

He kissed her, and an electric thrill raced up and down her spine. For a moment, she was so caught up in the kiss that she couldn't think. As the kiss ended, her dread returned. She spontaneously tightened her grip around his neck and hugged him as close as she could.

How could she ever leave him?

After a moment, Luke pulled back enough to see her face. "I've got something to show you. Come on."

He took her hand, and they strolled toward the woods on the other side of the lawn.

"Are we going on a hike?" Kaydi asked.

"Nope."

"Are we searching for mushrooms?"

"What?" Luke gave her a quizzical look. "No."

"Are we . . ." She searched her mind for another question to ask him.

"I want to show you a tree," he said before she could come up with something.

Kaydi swung her arm wide, and the rings on her fingers sparkled in the sunlight. "I see all kinds of trees. A forest of them."

"This is a very special tree. One you'll be especially interested in."

"Sounds mysterious."

Luke didn't reply, but a secretive smile flitted across his face. He quickened his pace as they neared a line of maples near a fence.

"Here it is," Luke announced, ushering her beneath the spreading branches of the chosen tree. The full canopy shaded them from the blazing heat of the June sun. He placed his hand on the trunk. "This is a message tree."

Kaydi listened, spellbound, as he told her about his grandmother's story of messages left in the tree, the scraps of lilac stationery covered in faded writing, and his own suppositions. She rested her hand on her heart. The story thrilled and pained her at the same time.

"We'll never know for sure who left the last message here," he concluded. "I think it's safe to say it was either my ancestor or yours."

"I think it must have been yours," she said. "Caroline may have written one last plea to my grandfather. Or perhaps she wrote to my grandmother."

"The letter was left unread."

"And abandoned." The poignant ache in Kaydi's heart deepened. "It makes you wonder if Caroline wrote the letter right before they eloped, then never returned to the tree at all."

"I wish I had kept the scraps, but they meant nothing to a kid who was hoping to find a treasure map." Luke shrugged. "I don't even remember throwing them away."

"Maybe you didn't," Kaydi said. "Maybe they're still there."

He shook his head. "They aren't." His tone became more upbeat. "Something else is."

"What?"

"Why don't you find out?" Luke suggested, pointing to the hole in the tree.

She eyed him with curiosity, then shifted her gaze to the tree. "You want me to reach into that hole? What if something bites me?"

He laughed. "Nothing will. I promise."

Kaydi stood on tiptoe to peer into the hole. It seemed to be lined with something. Maybe metal. Her heart flipped. A black ring box sat on a piece of folded cloth. She glanced back at Luke. He wasn't smiling or frowning, but hope shone in his eyes.

Could this really, truly be happening? It was what she wanted—with all her heart she wanted this moment. She picked up the box, cradling it in her hands as if it were something fragile.

"It's true we haven't known each other very long," Luke said, "but I don't need more time to know that I don't want to give my heart to anyone but you."

His words, the love in his eyes, enveloped her in a cocoon of belonging and dreams and possibilities. Kaydi wanted to throw herself into his arms, delete the boarding pass from the airline app on her phone, and never leave him.

"People will say we're being foolish," she hedged.

"They will."

"They'll say we'll be sorry."

Luke stepped closer and clasped her elbows in his hands. She still cradled the box, holding it between them.

"Then we'll prove them wrong," he said. "By loving each other the rest of our lives. By being the happiest couple in the whole world. By growing old together."

"We will." Kaydi opened the box and gasped at the lovely ring inside. How could he have known that this was exactly the kind of ring she would want? "Oh, Luke, it's so beautiful."

He smiled broadly as he took the ring from the box. "It belonged to my dad's grandmother. I hope you don't mind wearing it until we can go shopping."

"We don't need to go shopping." Kaydi slipped off all the rings on her left hand and shoved them into her pocket. "I'd be proud and delighted to wear your great-grandmother's ring."

He knelt down on one knee and took her left hand in his. "Kaydi-Paris Alexandria Engstrom, will you do me the honor of being my wife?"

"I will." Joyful tears sprang to her eyes as he slipped the antique ring onto her finger. She flung her arms around him, and they embraced.

Beneath the message tree, where letters of love and hope and perhaps regret had once been hidden, Kaydi and Luke sealed their betrothal with a long, romantic kiss.

30

Luke

Saying goodbye to Kaydi was one of the hardest things Luke had ever done, even though he reminded himself that he'd see her again the next day. He put her bags in her rental car early Sunday morning while she hugged Grace and Charlotte and promised to visit them again soon.

The two women had no idea how soon. As far as they knew, Kaydi was headed to Charleston to catch her flight to Omaha.

But Kaydi and Luke had other plans.

After Grace returned to the inn and Charlotte left for church, Luke gripped Kaydi's hands in his.

"We're really doing this," she said, her voice full of excitement.

"We really are," Luke said. "Are you sure you want to?"

"More than anything in the world."

They kissed one more time, a kiss neither of them was eager to end.

Kaydi climbed into her vehicle, and Luke got on his motorcycle. He followed her down the drive and waved as she turned right toward the interstate. Then he headed left in the direction of Foxsong Meadows.

Once he got home, he regarded the estate with fresh eyes. This place, big as it was and once considered the albatross around his neck, would always be his home. Now it would be Kaydi's home too. Though they would live in the gatehouse, they also planned to start the arduous process of going through the mansion's history, starting with the furniture, trunks, dressers, and boxes in the attic.

Luke changed clothes and went to work on the Townsend sculpture, but his mind wasn't on the vision he had for the piece. Instead, he pictured Kaydi driving her rental car to the first county seat she came to on the other side of the Georgia state line. There they could get a license and be married on the same day. Tomorrow.

Luke had to pinch himself to be sure he wasn't dreaming. He and Kaydi were eloping in secret. Just like Callie Jo Emmett and Joseph Piper all those years ago. And just like Kaydi's grandparents, they were deeply in love and always would be.

Sitting under the message tree yesterday, they had made their plans. Kaydi would travel to Georgia instead of home to Omaha. He would meet her there in the morning, and they'd go to the courthouse together. After the wedding, they'd drive to Savannah for their honeymoon.

A few days later they'd come back to Foxsong Meadows long enough for him to finish his current commissions and to host a reception for all their friends. Then they'd be on the road again, driving west to Omaha to visit Kaydi's family and then to wherever their wandering feet took them searching out the odd and the unusual—the treasures that other people saw as junk but the two of them viewed as artistic inspiration.

Luke couldn't imagine a happier life for him and the freckled brunette who'd stolen his heart.

31

Grace

Fresh flowers in all the suites? Check. Give Winston his heartworm medicine? Check. Order new napkins and place mats for the Fourth of July? Check.

Grace stood at the reception counter and marked each item off her to-do list with a satisfied flourish. The inn was fully booked for the upcoming Fourth of July holiday, and she wanted to have as many tasks completed as possible before the first guests arrived later that afternoon.

The bell at the front door chimed as Winnie entered with a stack of mail. "Are you too busy to take a little break?"

"I'd love one," Grace said.

"Good." Winnie placed the mail on the counter and handed Grace the top envelope. "I saw Charlotte outside. She went to her cottage to take a phone call from her publisher and asked me to be sure you saw this letter."

The return address was the Foxsong Meadows gatehouse. Grace removed a note card and two photos from the envelope. The picture showed Luke and Kaydi, arms around each other, standing in front of a courthouse. Kaydi wore a tea-length white dress and held a bouquet of golden daisies and pink tea roses. The second picture showed them standing in front of the Waving Girl statue located along Savannah's famed riverfront.

"Did you see these?" Grace handed the photos to her aunt.

"Apparently Kaydi didn't fly home after all." Winnie gestured toward the note. "Charlotte and I read it. Those two scamps eloped without telling a soul."

Grace read the note for herself, then smiled at her aunt. "Usually, I'd be worried about two young people running off to get married like that, but in this instance, I think they'll be extremely happy."

"So do I," Winnie agreed. "I'm so glad they'll be living at Foxsong Meadows. I've become quite fond of Kaydi and her different drummer."

Before Grace could respond, the chime sounded again as the door opened.

"We're back," Danielle said as she entered the foyer with Clayton beside her. "Hope you don't mind us stopping in like this."

"Of course we don't mind." Grace came around the counter, and the two women hugged. "I know you've only been gone a few days, but I've been on pins and needles ever since you left. How are you?"

"We couldn't be better." Danielle clasped Clayton's arm.

"We have news," he said. "We wanted to tell you in person."

Grace introduced Clayton to Winnie, then invited everyone to have a seat in the living room. Danielle and Clayton agreed while Winnie excused herself to continue her walk.

"I'll get us a snack," Grace said. She hurried to the kitchen and prepared a tray. She set chocolate chip cookies on a plate and poured three glasses of iced tea.

When Grace entered the living room, Danielle and Clayton were seated on one of the sofas. Grace handed the glasses to her guests and set the plate of cookies on the coffee table.

Winston ran into the room. The dog scampered over to Danielle and put his paws on her knee.

Danielle scratched the top of his head. "You haven't been playing with any more skunks, have you?"

"Thank heavens, no. Though I have the de-skunking concoction ready in case he ever does." Grace sat down in a nearby chair. "Now tell me your news."

Danielle and Clayton exchanged glances and smiled at each other.

"You go first," Danielle said to him.

"Okay, then." He turned to Grace. "Thanks to Spencer and his friend and a very good lawyer, we have been completely cleared of any wrongdoing."

"That's wonderful," Grace said. "What happened?"

"Conrad, the restaurant's chief financial officer, finally confessed and named his accomplice," Clayton replied.

"The accomplice was a security guard at Maddox Creative," Danielle put in. "Conrad bribed him to pull out the winning tickets after he picked them up from the printing company."

"Why?" Grace asked.

"He wanted to be sure no one claimed the grand prize," Clayton explained. "The chain isn't as solvent as he's been leading the board to believe."

"He's been embezzling," Danielle added. "From his own family."

"That's awful," Grace said. "Why would he do that?"

"Apparently he'd gotten in over his head with credit card debt." Clayton selected a chocolate chip cookie. "His oldest daughter was accepted into a top-notch private school, and he didn't want to tell her that he couldn't afford the tuition."

"So he rigged a sweepstakes and framed an innocent man." Grace shook her head. How could anyone do such a thing?

"He was desperate," Clayton said as if he'd read her thought. "Desperate people do desperate things."

"Like run away and hide in a small town." Danielle lightly tapped Clayton's elbow with hers.

"I'm glad that's what we did." He took Danielle's hand. "For more reasons than one."

"Now for our other news." Danielle smiled at Grace. "We're moving out west to open that boutique marketing firm we talked about. We're also getting married."

Grace clasped her hands together. "Oh, I'm so thrilled for both of you. When's the wedding?"

"In two weeks." Danielle's eyes glowed with happiness. "We're only inviting a few people, and we're hoping you and Spencer will come."

At the sound of Spencer's name, a knot formed in Grace's stomach. How could she attend a wedding with him? If Danielle knew their history, she'd never have asked such a thing. But she didn't know, and Grace didn't have the words to try to explain.

"I can't speak for Spencer," she said, then stopped to clear her throat. "But I wouldn't miss it for the world."

Danielle and Clayton shared more of their plans with Grace, and she told them about Kaydi and Luke's elopement.

Grace smiled as she thought of how the Magnolia Harbor Inn had worked its magic once again by bringing these two special couples together.

When it was time for Danielle and Clayton to leave, Grace walked with them to their car and waved goodbye as they drove away.

She was standing on the veranda with Winston at her feet when Charlotte appeared. "Something wrong?" Charlotte asked, reading her sister's face as accurately as she always did.

"I'm fine." Grace gave her a hug. "Just deep in thought."

"Care to share?"

"I was thinking of Mr. and Mrs. Brannick." *Young love.* "And the soon-to-be Clayton and Danielle Lowe." *Grown-up love.* She truly was happy for the two couples.

"Were they here?" Charlotte exclaimed. "They're getting married? When's the wedding? What happened with the sweepstakes? I wish I had been here."

The rush of questions pulled Grace from her thoughts. Instead of answering any of them, she laughed. *Sister love. What could be better?*

Grace was overcome with thankfulness for her sister and their wonderful life at the inn. She was blessed to have such an amazing family, a sweet dog, and loyal friends. No matter what happened with Spencer, Grace knew that she had the support of her family and friends and she'd be all right.

Suddenly, Winston trotted to the edge of the veranda and barked.

Grace gazed across the yard as a black-and-white animal streaked toward the nearest trees.

Winston jumped from the porch to give chase.

"Winston, no!" the sisters shouted at the same time.

The little dog ignored their shouts in his pursuit of the odoriferous intruder.

If nothing else, this life was never dull, and Grace wouldn't even exchange the skunks for anything in the world.